Nicholasa Mohr

Rituals of Survival:
A Woman's Portfolio

C. Golpe and Lisa E. Davis
ping me complete this portfolio of stories.

The publication of this volume is made possible through a grant from the National Endowment for the Arts, a federal agency.

The paper used in this publication meets the minimum requirements of the American National Standard for Permanence of Paper for Printed Library Materials Z39.48-1984. ∞

Second Printing, 1986
Third Printing, 1990

Arte Publico Press
University of Houston
University Park
Houston, Texas 77004

ISBN 0-934770-39-5
Library of Congress No. 84-072300

To the memory of Evelina Lopez Antonetty, a beloved and valiant sister.

CONTENTS

Aunt Rosana's Rocker

(Zoraida)

Aunt Rosana's Rocker
(Zoraida)

Casto paced nervously, but softly, the full length of the small kitchen, then quietly, he tiptoed across the kitchen threshhold into the living room. After going a few feet, he stopped to listen. The sounds were getting louder. Casto returned to the kitchen, switched on the light, and sat down trying to ignore what he heard. But the familiar sounds were coming directly from their bedroom where Zoraida was. They grew louder as they traveled past the tiny foyer, the living room and into the kitchen, which was the room furthest away from her.

Leaning forward, Casto stretched his hands out palms down on the kitchen table. Slowly he made two fists, squeezing tightly, and watched as his knuckles popped out tensely under his skin. He could almost feel her presence there, next to him, panting and breathing heavily. The panting developed into moans of sensual pleasure, disrupting the silence of the apartment.

"If only I could beat someone!" Casto whispered hoarsely, banging his fists against the table and upsetting the sugar bowl. The cover slipped off the bowl, landed on its side and rolled toward the edge of the table. Casto waited for it to drop to the floor, anticipating a loud crash, but the cover stopped right at the very edge and fell quietly and flatly on the table, barely making a sound.

He looked up at the electric clock on the wall over the refrigerator; it was two-thirty in the morning.

Again, Casto tried not to listen and concentrated instead on the night noises outside in the street. Traffic on the avenue had almost completely disappeared. Occasionally, a car sped by; someone's footsteps echoed against the pavement, and off at a distance, he heard a popular tune being whistled. Casto instinctively hummed along until the sound slipped away, and he then realized he was shivering. The old radiators had stopped clanking and hissing earlier; they were now ice cold. He remembered that the landlord never sent up heat after ten at night. He wished he had thought to bring a sweater or blanket with him; he was afraid of catching a cold. But he would not go back inside; instead, he opened his special section of the cupboard and searched among his countless bottles of vitamins and nutrient supplements until he found the jar of natural vitamin C tablets. He popped several tablets into his mouth and sat down, resigned to the fact that he would rather stay here, where he felt safe, even at the risk of getting a chill. This was as far away as he could get from her, without leaving the apartment.

The sounds had now become louder and more intense. Casto raised his hands and covered his ears. He shut his eyes trying not to imagine what she was doing now. But with each sound, he could clearly see her in her ecstasy. Casto recalled how he had jumped out of bed in a fright the first time it had happened. Positive that she had gone into convulsions, he had stood almost paralyzed at a safe distance looking down at her. He didn't know what to do. And, as he helplessly watched her, his stomach had suddenly turned ice-cold with fear. Zoraida seemed to be another person. She was stretched out on the bed pulling at the covers; turning, twisting her body and rocking her buttocks sensually. Her knees had been bent upward with her legs far apart and she had thrust her pelvis forward forcefully and rhythmically. Zoraida's head was pushed back and her mouth open, as she licked her lips, moaning and gasping with excitement. Casto remembered Zoraida's eyes when she had opened them for brief moments. They had been fixed on someone or something, as if beckoning; but there was no one and certainly nothing he could see in the darkness of the room. She had rolled back the pupils and only the whites of her eyes were visible. She had blinked rapidly, shutting her eyes and twitching her nose and mouth. Then, a smile had passed her lips and a stream of saliva had run down her chin, neck and chest.

Now, as he heard low moans filled with pleasure, interrupted by short painful yelps that pierced right through him, Casto could also imagine her every gesture.

Putting down his hands, Casto opened his eyes. All he could do was wait patiently, as he always did, wait for her to finish. Maybe tonight won't be a long one; Casto swallowed anxiously.

He remembered about the meeting he had arranged earlier in the evening without Zoraida's knowledge, and felt better. After work, he had gone to see his mother; then they had both gone to see Zoraida's parents. It had been difficult for him to speak about it, but he had managed somehow to tell them everything. At first they had reacted with disbelief, but after he had explained carefully and in detail what was happening, they had understood his embarrassment and his reluctance to discuss this with anyone. He told them that when it all had begun, he was positive Zoraida was reacting to a high fever and was simply dreaming, perhaps even hallucinating. But, it kept happening, and it soon developed into something that occurred frequently, almost every night.

He finally realized something or someone had taken a hold of her. He was sure she was not alone in that room and in that bed!

It was all bizarre and, unless one actually saw her, he explained, it was truly beyond belief. Why, her actions were lewd and vulgar, and if they were sexual, as it seemed, then this was not the kind of sex a decent husband and wife engage in. What was even harder for him to bear was her enjoyment. Yes, this was difficult, watching her total enjoyment of this whole disgusting business! And, to make matters more compli-cated, the next day, Zoraida seemed to remember nothing. In fact, during the day, she was normal again. Perhaps a bit more tired than usual, but then, who wouldn't be after such an exhausting ordeal? And, lately she had become even less talkative with him, almost silent. But, make no mistake, Casto assured them, Zoraida remained a wonderful housekeeper and devoted mother. Supper was served on time, chores were done without fuss, the apartment was immaculate, and the kids were attended to without any problems. This happened only at night, or rather early in the morning, at about two or two-thirty. He had not slept properly since this whole affair started. After all, he had to drive out to New Jersey to earn his living and his strength and sleep were being sapped away. He had even considered sleeping on the living room couch, but he would not be driven out of his own bed. He was still a man after all, a macho, master of his home, someone to be reckoned with, not be pushed out!

Trying to control his anger, Casto had confessed that it had been a period of almost two months since he had normal and natural relations with his wife. He reminded them that he, as a man, had his needs, and this would surely make him ill, if it continued. Of course, he would not touch her . . . not as she was right now. After all, he reasoned, who knows what he could catch from her? As long as she was under the control of some- thing — whatever it might be — he would keep his distance. No, Casto told them, he wanted no part of their daughter as a woman, not as long as she remained in this condition.

When her parents had asked him what Zoraida had to say about all of this, Casto had laughed, answering that she knew even less about it than he did. In fact, at one point she did not believe him and had sworn on the children's souls, claiming her innocence. But Casto had persisted and now Zoraida had finally believed him. She felt that she might be the victim of something, perhaps a phenomenon. Who knows? When Zoraida's parents and his mother suggested a consultation with Doña Digna, the spiritualist, he had quickly agreed.

Casto jumped slightly in his chair as he heard loud passionate moans and deep groans emanate from the bedroom and fill the kitchen.

"Stop it . . . stop, you bitch!" Casto clenched his teeth, spitting out the words. But he took care not to raise his voice. "Stop it! What a happy victim you are! Puta! Whore! Some phenomenon . . . I don't believe you and your story." But, even as he said these words, Casto knew he was not quite sure what to believe.

The first loud thump startled Casto and he braced himself and waited, anticipating what was to come. He heard the legs on their large double bed pounding the floor as the thumping became louder and faster.

Casto shuddered and folded his arms, digging his fingers into the flesh of his forearms. After a few moments, he finally heard her release, one long cry followed by several grunts, and then silence. He relaxed and sighed deeply with relief; it was all over.

"Animal . . . she's just like an animal, no better than an alley cat in heat." Casto was wet with cold perspiration. He was most frightened of this last part. "Little hypocrite!"

Casto rememberd how she always urged him to hurry, be quiet, and get it over with, on account of the children. A lot she cares about him tonight! Never in all their years of marriage had she ever uttered such sounds — he shook his head — or shown any passion or much interest in doing it.

Casto looked up at the clock; it was two minutes to three. He thought about the noise, almost afraid to move, fearful that his downstairs neighbor Roberto might knock on the door any moment. He recalled how Roberto had called him aside one morning and spoken to him, "Two and three in the morning, my friend; can't you and your wife control your passions at such an ungodly hour? My God . . . such goings on! Man, and to tell you the truth, you people up there get me all worked up and horny. Then, when I touch my old lady, she won't cooperate at that time, eh?" He had poked Casto playfully and winked, "Hey, what am I gonna do? Have a heart, friend." Casto shook his head, how humiliating and so damned condescending. They were behaving like the most common, vulgar people. Soon the whole fucking building would know! Roberto Thomas and his big mouth! Yes, and what will that sucker say to me next time? Casto trembled with anger. He wanted to rush in and shake Zoraida, wake her, beat her; he wanted to demand an explanation or else! But, he knew it wouldn't do any good. Twice he had tried. The first time, he had spoken to her the following day. The second time, he had tried to wake her up and she had only become wilder with him, almost violent, scaring him out of the bedroom. Afterwards, things had only become worse. During the day she withdrew, practically not speaking one word to him. The next few nights she had become wilder and the ordeal lasted even longer. No, he could not confront her.

Casto realized all was quiet again. He shut off the light, then stood and slowly, with trepidation, walked through the living room and entered the small foyer leading to their bedroom. He stopped before the children's bedroom, and carefully turned the knob partially opening the door. All three were fast asleep. He was grateful they never woke up. What could he say to them? That their mother was sick? But sick with what?

As he stood at the entrance of their bedroom, Casto squinted scrutinizing every corner of the room before entering. The street lights seeping through the venetian blinds dimly illuminated the overcrowded bedroom. All was peaceful and quiet; nothing was disturbed or changed in any visible way. Satisfied, he walked in and looked down at Zoraida. She was fast asleep, breathing deeply and evenly, a look of serene contentment covered her face. Her long dark hair was spread over the pillow and spilled out onto the covers. Casto was struck by her radiant appearance each time it was all over. She had an air of glamour, so strange in a woman as plain as Zoraida. He realized, as he continued to stare at her, that he was frightened of Zoraida. He wanted to laugh at himself, but when Zoraida turned her head slightly, Casto found himself backing out of the room.

Casto stood at the entrance and whispered, "Zoraida, nena . . . are . . . are you awake?" She did not stir. Casto waited perfectly still and kept his eyes on her. After a few moments, Casto composed himself. He was sure she would remain sleeping; she had never woken up after it was all over. Slowly, he entered the room and inched his way past the bulky bureau, the triple dresser and the rocking chair near the window, finally reaching his side of the bed.

Casto rapidly made the sign of the cross before he lay down beside Zoraida. He was not very religious, he could take it or leave it; but, now, he reasoned that by crossing himself he was on God's side.

Casto glanced at the alarm clock; there were only two-and-a-half hours of sleep left before starting the long trip out to the docks of Bayonne, New Jersey. God, he was damned tired; he hardly ever got enough sleep anymore. This shit had to stop! Never mind, wait until the meeting. He remembered that they were all going to see Doña Digna, the spiritualist. That ought to change things. He smiled and felt some comfort knowing that this burden would soon be lifted. Seconds later he shut his eyes and fell fast asleep.

Everyone finished supper. Except for the children's chatter and Junior's protests about finishing his food, it had been a silent meal.

Casto got up and opened his special section of the cupboard. The children watched the familiar ritual without much interest as their father set out several jars of vitamins, two bottles of iron and liver tonic and a small plastic box containing therapeutic tablets. Casto carefully counted out and popped an assortment of twenty-four vitamin tablets into his mouth and then took several spoonfuls of tonic. He carefully examined the contents of the plastic box and decided not to take any of those tablets.

"Okay, Clarita, today you take vitamin C . . . and two multi-vitamin supplements. You, too, Eddie and Junior, you might as well . . ."

The children accepted the vitamins he gave them without resistance or fuss. They knew by now that no one could be excused from the table until Casto had finished taking and dispensing vitamins and tonic.

"Okay, kids, that's it. You can all have dessert later when your grandparents get here."

Quickly the children left.

Although Casto often suggested that Zoraida should eat properly, he had never asked her to take any of his vitamins or tonic, and she had never expressed either a desire or interest to do so.

He looked at Zoraida as she worked clearing the table and putting things away. Zoraida felt her heart pounding fiercely and she found it difficult to breathe. She wanted him to stop staring at her like that. Lately she found his staring unbearable. Zoraida's shyness had always determined her behavior in life. Ever since she could remember, any attempt that others made at intimate conversations or long discussions created feelings of constraint, developing into such anxiety that when she spoke, her voice had a tendency to fade. This was a constant problem for her; people often asked, "What was that?" or "Did you say something?" These feelings extended even into her family life. When her children asked impertinent questions, she would blush, unable to answer. Zoraida was ashamed of her own nakedness with Casto and would only undress when he was not present. When her children chanced to see her undressed at an unguarded moment, she would be distraught for several days.

It had been Casto's self assurance and his ability to be aggressive and determined with others that had attracted her to him.

Casto looked at Zoraida as she worked. "I'll put my things back and get the coffee started for when they get here," he said. She nodded and continued swiftly and silently with her chores.

Zoraida was twenty-eight, and although she had borne four children (three living, one still-born) and had suffered several miscarriages, she was of slight build and thin, with narrow hips. She had a broad face and her smile revealed a wide space between her two front teeth. As a result, she appeared frail and childlike, much younger than her years. Whenever she was tired, dark circles formed under her eyes, contrasting against the paleness of her skin. This evening, she seemed to look even paler than ever to Casto; almost ghostlike.

Casto was, by nature, hypochondriacal and preoccupied with avoiding all sorts of diseases. He was tall and robust, with a broad frame; in fact, he was the picture of good health. He became furious when others laughed at him for taking so many vitamins and health foods. Most people ignored his pronouncements of ill health and even commented behind his back. "Casto'll live to be one hundred if he lives a day . . . why, he's as fit as an ox! It's Zoraida who should take all them vitamins and then complain some. She looks like a toothpick, una flaca! That woman has nothing to show. I wonder what Casto ever saw in her, eh?"

Yet, it was her frail and sickly appearance that had attracted him the first time he saw her. He was visiting his married sister, Purencia, when Zoraida had walked in with her friend, Anna. Anna was a beautiful, voluptuous young woman with an olive tone to her skin that glowed; and when she smiled, her white teeth and full lips made her appear radiant. Zoraida, thin and pale by contrast, looked ill. In Casto's presence, she had smiled sheepishly, blushing from time to time. Anna had flirted openly, and commented on Purencia's brother, "You didn't tell me you had such a gorgeous macho in your family. Trying to keep him a secret, girl?" But it had been Zoraida that he was immediately drawn to. Casto had been so taken with her that he had confided in a friend that very day, "She really got to me, you know? Not loud or vulgar like that other girl, who was acting like a man, making remarks about me and all. No, she was a real lady. And, she's like, well, like a little sick sparrow flirting with death and having the upper hand. Quietly stubborn, you know? Not at all submissive like it might seem to just anybody looking at Zoraida. It's more as if nobody's gonna make the sparrow healthy, but it ain't gonna die either . . . like it's got the best of both worlds, see?"

Yet, in all their nine years of marriage, Zoraida had never become seriously ill. Her pregnancies and miscarriages were the only time that she had been unable to attend to her family. After the last pregnancy, in an attempt to prevent children, Casto had decided on the rhythm system, where abstention is practiced during certain days of the month. It was, he reasoned, not only sanctioned by the Catholic Church, but there were no drugs or foreign objects put into one's body, and he did not have to be afraid of catching something nor getting sick.

Even after this recent miscarriage, Zoraida appeared to recover quickly, and with her usual amazing resiliency, managed the household chores and the children all by herself. She even found time to assuage Casto's fears of sickness and prepare special foods for him.

Casto could feel his frustration building inside as he watched her. What the hell was the matter with this wife of his? Quickly he reached into his cupboard and took out some Maalox; God, the last thing he wanted was an ulcer on account of all of this.

"I think I'll coat my stomach." Casto chewed several Maalox tablets vigorously, then swallowed. "This way, I can have coffee later and it won't affect me badly." He waited for a response, but she remained silent. Casto sighed, she don't even talk to me no more . . . well, that's why I invited everybody here tonight, so they could see for themselves! He waited, staring at her, and then asked, "You got the cakes ready? I mean, you got them out of the boxes and everything?"

Zoraida nodded, not looking in his direction.

"Hey! Coño, I'm talking to you! Answer!"

"Yes," Zoraida whispered.

"And the cups and plates, you got them for the coffee and cake?"

"Yes," Zoraida repeated.

"I don't know, you know? It's been almost three months since Doña Digna did her job and cured you. I didn't figure you were gonna get so . . . so depressed." Zoraida continued to work silently. "Wait. Stop a minute. Why don't you answer me, eh? Will you look at me, for God's sake!"

Zoraida stopped and faced Casto with her eyes lowered.

"Look, I'm trying to talk to you, understand? Can't you talk to me?" Zoraida kept perfectly still. "Say something, will you?"

"What do you want me to say?" Zoraida spoke softly, without looking at him.

"Can't you look at me when you talk?"

Swiftly and furtively, Zoraida glanced at Casto, then lowered her eyes once more.

"Coño, man, what do you think I do all day out there to make a living? Play? Working my butt off in those docks in all kinds of weather . . . yeah. And for what? To come home to a woman that won't even look at me?" Casto's voice was loud and angry. He stopped, controlled himself, then continued, lowering his voice. "I get up every morning before six. Every freaking morning! I risk pneumonia, rheumatism, arthritis, all kinds of sickness. Working that fork lift, eight, ten hours a day, until my kidneys feel like they're gonna split out of my sides. And then, to make it worse, I gotta take orders from that stupid foreman who hates Puerto Ricans. Calling me a spic. In fact, they all hate Puerto Ricans out there. They call me spic, and they get away with it because I'm the only P.R. there, you know? Lousy Micks and Dagos! Listen, you know what they . . . ah, what's the use, I can't talk to you. Sure, why should you care? All you do is stay in a nice apartment, all warm and cozy. Damn it! I can't even have my woman like a normal man. First you had a phantom lover, right? Then, ever since Doña Digna took him away, you have that lousy chair you sit in and do your disappearing act. That's all you're good for lately. I can't even come near you. The minute I approach you like a human being for normal sex, you go and sit in that . . . that chair! I seen you fade out. Don't think I'm blind. You sit in that freaking thing, rocking away. You look . . . you . . . I don't even think you're breathing when you

sit there! You should see yourself. What you look like is enough
to scare anybody. Staring into space like some God damned
zombie! You know what I should do with it? Throw it out, or
better yet, bust that piece of crap into a thousand splinters! Yeah,
that's what I ought to do. Only thing is, you'll find something
else, right? Another lover, is that what you want, so you can
become an animal? Because with me, let me tell you, you ain't
no animal. With me you're nothing. Mira, you know something,
I'm not taking no more of this. Never mind, when they get here
they can see your whole bullshit act for themselves. Especially
after I tell them . . ."

Zoraida barely heard him. The steady sound of the television
program and the children's voices coming from their bedroom
filled her with a pleasant feeling. How nice, she thought, all the
children playing and happy. All fed and clean; yes, it's nice and
peaceful.

The front doorbell rang.

"There they are." Casto had finished preparing the coffee.
"I'll answer the door, you go on and get things ready."

Zoraida heard voices and trembled as she remembered Casto's threats and the fury he directed at her. Now he was going to
tell them all sorts of things about her . . . untruths.

"Zoraida, where are you?" She heard her mother's voice,
and then the voices of her father, mother-in-law and sister-in-
law.

"Mommy, Mommy," Clarita ran into the kitchen, "Nana and
Granpa, and Abuelita and Titi Purencia are here. Can we have
the cake now?"

"In a little while, Clarita." Zoraida followed her daughter out
into the living room and greeted everybody.

"Mommy, Mommy!" Junior shouted, "Tell Eddie to stop it,
he's hitting me!"

"I was not, it was Clarita!" Eddie walked over to his little
brother and pushed him. Junior began to cry and Clarita ran over
and smacked Eddie.

"See?" Casto shouted, "Stop it! Clarita, you get back inside." He jumped up, grabbing his daughter by an elbow and lifting her off the ground. "Demonia, why are you hitting him? Zoraida, can't you control these kids?" He shook Clarita forcefully and she began to whine.

"Casto," Zoraida's thin shriek whistled through the room. "Don't be rough with her, please!"

"See that, Doña Clara, your daughter can't even control her own kids no more." He turned to the children, "Now, all of you, get back inside your room and watch television; and be quiet or you go right to bed and nobody gets any cake. You hear? That means all three, Clarita, Eddie and you too Junior."

"Can we have the cake now?" Eddie asked.

"I'll call you when it's time. Now go on, go on, all of you." Quickly, the children left.

"Calm yourself, son." Doña Elvira, Casto's mother, walked over to him. "You know how children are, they don't know about patience or waiting; you were no angel yourself, you and your sister."

"Let's go inside and have coffee, everybody." Casto led them into the kitchen. There were six chairs set around the kitchen table. Doña Clara and her husband, Don Isidro, Doña Elvira and her daughter, Purencia, squeezed in and sat down.

"Cut some cake for the kids and I'll bring it in to them," Casto spoke to Zoraida, who quickly began to cut up the chocolate cake and place the pieces on a plate. Everyone watched in silence. "Milk," snapped Casto. Zoraida set out three glasses of milk. Casto put everything on a tray and left.

"So, mi hijita, how are you?" Doña Clara asked her daughter.

"I'm okay." Zoraida sat down.

"You look pale to me, very pale. Don't she, Papa?" Doña Clara turned for a moment to Don Isidro, then continued without waiting for an answer. "You're probably not eating right. Zoraida, you have to take better care of yourself."

"All right." Casto returned and sat down with the others.

"They're happy now."

"Son," Doña Elvira spoke to Casto. "You look tired, aren't you getting enough rest?"

"I'm all right, Ma. Here, everybody, have some cake and coffee."

Everyone began to help themselves.

"It's that job of his. He works so hard," Doña Elvira reached over and placed an extra large piece of chocolate cake on Casto's plate before continuing, "He should have stayed in school and become an accountant, like I wanted. Casto was so good at math, but . . . instead, he . . ."

"Pass the sugar, please," Doña Clara interrupted, "and a little bit of that rum cake, yes. Thank you."

They all ate in silence.

Doña Elvira looked at Zoraida and sighed, trying to hide her annoyance. What a sickly looking woman, bendito. She looks like a mouse. To think my handsome, healthy son, who could have had any girl he wanted, picked this one. Doña Elvira could hardly swallow her cake. Duped by her phony innocence is what it was! And how could he be happy and satisfied with such a woman? Look at her, she's pathetic. Now, oh yes, now, he's finding out who she really is: not the sweet innocent one, after all! Ha! First a phantom lover and now . . . who knows what! Well, we'll see how far she can go on with this, because now he's getting wise. With a sense of smug satisfaction, Doña Elvira half-smiled as she looked at her daughter-in-law, then ate her cake and drank her coffee.

Purencia saw her mother's look of contempt directed at Zoraida. She's jealous of Zoraida, Purencia smiled. Nobody was ever good enough for Casto. For her precious baby boy, well, and there you have it! Casto finally wanted Zoraida. Purencia smiled, serves Ma right. She looked at her sister-in-law who sat with her head bowed. God, she looks sicker than ever, but she never complains. She won't say nothing, even now, when he's putting her through this whole number. Poor goody-two-shoes

Zoraida, she's not gonna get on Casto's case for nothing; like, why is he jiving her? I wonder what it is she's doing now? After that whole scene with Doña Digna, I thought she cured her of whatever that was. Purencia shrugged, who knows how it is with these quiet ones. They're the kind that hide the action. Maybe she's doing something nobody knows about . . . well, let's just see.

Doña Clara looked at her son-in-law, Casto, with anger and a scowl on her face. Bestia . . . brute of a man! He doesn't deserve anyone as delicate as Zoraida. She has to wait on that huge monster hand and foot. With all his stupid medicines and vitamins when he's as fit as a horse! Ungrateful man. He got an innocent girl, pure as the day she was born, that's what. Protected and brought up right by us. Never went out by herself. We always watched out who her friends were. She was guarded by us practically up until the moment she took her vows. Any man would have been proud to have her. Canalla! Sinvergüenza! She's clean, hardworking and obedient. Never complains. All he wants to do is humiliate her. We already went to Doña Digna, and Casto said Zoraida was cured. What now, for pity's sake? Doña Clara forced herself to turn away from Casto because the anger fomenting within her was beginning to upset her nerves.

Don Isidro sat uneasily. He wished his wife would not drag him into these things. Domestic disputes should be a private matter, he maintained emphatically, between man and wife. But, his wife's nerves were not always what they should be, and so he had to be here. He looked at his daughter and was struck by her girlish appearance. Don Isidro sighed, the mother of three children and she hasn't filled out . . . she still has the body of a twelve-year old. Well, after all, she was born premature, weighing only two pounds at birth. Don Isidro smiled, remembering what the doctors had called her. "The miracle baby," they had said, "Mr. Cuesta, your daughter is a miracle. She should not be alive." That's when he and Clara had decided to give her the middle name of Milagros. He had wanted a son, but after

Zoraida's birth, his wife could bear no children, and so he had to be satisfied with what he had. Of course, he had two grandsons, but they wouldn't carry on his last name, so, in a way it was not the same. Well, she's lucky to be married at all. Don Isidro nodded slightly, and Casto is a good, honest, hardworking man, totally devoted. Don't drink or gamble; he don't even look at other women. But, he too was lucky to get our Zoraida. After all, we brung her up proper and right. Catholic schools. Decent friends. Don Isidro looked around him at the silent table and felt a stiffness in his chest. He took a deep breath; what had she done? This whole business confused him. He thought Doña Digna had made the situation right once more.

"So, Casto, how are you? How's work?" Don Isidro asked.

"Pretty good. The weather gets to me, though. I have to guard against colds and sitting in that fork-lift gives me a sore back. But, I'm lucky to have work, the way things are going."

"You're right, they're laying off people everywhere. You read about it in the news everyday."

"Zoraida, eat something," Doña Clara spoke to her daughter.

"I'm not hungry, Mami," Zoraida's voice was just above a whisper.

"Casto, you should see to it that she eats!" Doña Clara looked at her son-in-law, trying to control her annoyance. "Whatever this problem is, I'm sure part of it is that your wife never eats."

"Why should he see that she eats or not?" Doña Elvira interjected, "He has to go to work everyday to support his family . . . he hasn't got time to . . ."

"Wait a minute, Ma," Casto interrupted, "the problem here ain't food. That's not gonna solve what's going on."

"It seems to solve all your problems, eh?" Doña Clara looked at Casto with anger.

"Just hold on now . . . wait," Don Isidro raised his hand. Now, we are all arguing here with each other and we don't even know what the problem is. Why don't we find out what's going on?" Don Isidro turned to Casto and waited.

Everyone fell silent. Don Isidro continued, "I thought that Doña Digna's treatment worked. After all, you told us that yourself."

"It's not that no more," Casto looked around him, "it's something else now."

"What?" Doña Elvira asked.

Casto looked at Zoraida who sat with her hands folded on her lap and her eyes downcast.

"Weren't things going good for you two?" Don Isidro asked. "I mean, things were back to normal relations between you, yes?"

"Yes and no," Casto said. "Yes for a while and then . . ."

"Then what?" Doña Elvira asked. "What?"

Casto looked at Zoraida. "You want to say something, Zoraida?" She shook her head without looking at anyone.

"All right, then like usual, I gotta speak. You know that rocking chair Zoraida has? The one she brought with her when we got married?"

"You mean the one she's had ever since she was little? Why, we had that since Puerto Rico, it belonged to my titi Rosana." Doña Clara looked perplexed. "What about the rocker?"

"Well, she just sits in it, when . . . when she shouldn't." Casto could feel the blood rushing to his face.

"What do you mean she sits in it?" Doña Clara asked. "What is she supposed to do? Stand in it?"

"I said *when she shouldn't.*"

"Shouldn't what?" Doña Clara turned to Don Isidro, "Papa, what is this man talking about?"

"Look," Casto continued, "this here chair is in the bedroom. That's where she keeps it. All right? Now when, when I . . . when we . . ." Casto hesitated, "you know what I mean. Then, instead of acting like a wife, she leaves the bed and sits in the chair. She sits and she rocks back and forth.

"Does she stay there all night?" Doña Elvira asked.

"Pretty much."

Everyone looked at Zoraida, who remained motionless without lifting her eyes. A few moments passed before Don Isidro broke the silence.

"This is a delicate subject, I don't know if it's a good thing to have this kind of discussion here, like this."

"What do you want me to do, Isidro?" First she has those fits in bed driving me nuts. Then we call in Doña Digna, who decides she knows what's wrong, and puts me through a whole freakin rigamarole of prayers and buying all kinds of crap. After all of that pendejá, which costs me money that I frankly don't have, then she tells me my wife is cured. Now it starts again, except in another way. Look, I'm only human, you know? And she," Casto pointed to Zoraida, "is denying me what is my right as a man and as her husband. And I don't know why she's doing this. But I do know this time you're gonna be here to know what's going on. I ain't going through this alone. No way. And get myself sick? No!"

"Just a moment, now," Doña Clara said, "you say Zoraida sits in the rocker when you . . . approach her. Does she ever sit there at other times? Or only at that time?"

"Once in a while, at other times, but always . . . always, you know, at that time!"

"Ay . . . Dios mio!" Doña Elvira stood up. "I don't know how my son puts up with this, if you ask me." She put her hands to her head. "Casto has the patience of a saint, any other man would do . . . do worse!"

"What do you mean, the patience of a saint?" Doña Clara glared at Doña Elvira. "And do worse what? Your son might be the whole cause of this, for all I know . . ."

"Now, wait." Don Isidro stood up. "Again, we are fighting and blaming this one or that one. This will get us nowhere. Doña Elvira, please sit down." Doña Elvira sat, and then Don Isidro sat down also. "Between a man and wife, it's best not to interfere."

"Okay then, Papa, what are we here for?" Doña Clara asked.

"To help, if we can," Purencia spoke. Everyone listened; she had not spoken a word before this. "I think that's what my brother wants. Right, Casto?" Casto nodded, and then shrugged. "Let Zoraida say something," Purencia continued. "She never gets a chance to say one word."

"Nobody's stopping her." Casto looked at Zoraida. "Didn't I ask her to say something? In fact, maybe she can tell us what's going on. Like, I would like to know too, you know."

"Zoraida," Doña Clara spoke firmly to her daughter, "mira, you better tell us what all of this is about."

Zoraida looked up, meeting her mother's angry stare. "I don't know what Casto means about the chair."

"Do you sit in the rocker or do you not sit there, like he says?" Her mother asked.

"Sometimes."

"Sometimes? What times? Is it like the way he says it is? Because, if this is so, we want to know why. Doña Digna told me, you and all of us, that there was an evil spirit in you that was turning your thoughts away from your husband, so that you could not be a wife to him. After she finished her treatment, she said the evil spirit or force was gone, and that you would go back to a normal husband-and-wife relationship. We have to accept that. She is a woman of honor that has been doing this work for many years, and that she is telling us the truth, yes?" Doña Clara took a deep breath. "But, if you feel anything is wrong, then it could be that Doña Digna did not succeed." She turned to Casto. "That's possible too, you know. These things sometimes get very complicated. I remember when the Alvarez household was having the worst kind of luck. Don Pablo had lost his job, his wife was sick, and one of their boys had an accident; all kinds of problems, remember? You remember, Papa? Well, Doña Digna had to go back, and it took her a long time to discover the exact cause and then to make things straight again." She turned to Zoraida, "Bueno, mi hija, you have to tell us what you feel, and if you are doing this to your husband, why." Doña Clara waited for her daughter's response. "Go ahead. Answer, por Dios!"

"I..." Zoraida cleared her throat in an effort to speak louder. "I just sit in the rocker sometimes. Because I feel relaxed there."

"Yeah!" Casto said, "Every time I go near her at night, or at two or three in the morning, she relaxes." He raised his hand and slammed the table, "God damned chair!"

"Calmate, mi hijito, calm yourself." Doña Elvira put her hand over her eyes. "I don't know how long my son can put up with all of this. Now she's got an obsession with a chair. Virgen, purisima! Somebody has to tell me what is going on here!"

"Listen to me," Don Isidro spoke in a firm voice, "if it's the chair that bothers you, then we'll take it back home with us. Right, Mama?" He turned to Doña Clara who nodded emphatically. "There should be no objection to that, eh?"

Everyone looked at Casto who shrugged, and then at Zoraida who opened her mouth and shook her head, but was unable to speak.

"Very good." Don Isidro clasped his hands and smiled. "There, that ought to take care of the problems pretty much."

"Except, she might find something else." Casto said "Who knows with her."

"Well, but we don't know that for sure, do we?" Don Isidro replied "and in the meantime, we gotta start somewhere."

"I feel we can always call Doña Digna in again if we have to." Doña Clara poured herself a cup of coffee. "After all, she was the one that told us Zoraida was cured."

"I agree," Doña Elvira said, "and even though she don't ask for money, I know my Casto was very generous with her."

"That's right, they don't charge, but after all, one has to give these people something, or else how can they live?" agreed Doña Clara.

"Isn't the weather funny this Spring?" Doña Elvira spoke amiably. "One minute it's cold and the next it's like summer. One never knows how to dress these . . ."

They continued speaking about the weather and about television programs. Purencia spoke about her favorite movie.

"That one about the professional hit-man, who has a contract out to kill the President of England . . . no, France, I think. Anyway, remember when he goes into that woman's house and kills her? I was so scared, I loved that movie."

Everyone agreed, the best kinds of movies were mysteries and thrillers.

Zoraida half-listened to them. They were going to take away the rocker. She had always had it, ever since she could remember. When she was a little girl, her parents told her it was a part of their history. Part of Puerto Rico and her great Aunt Rosana who was very beautiful and had countless suitors. The chair was made of oak with intricate carving and delicate caning. As a little girl, Zoraida used to rub her hands against the caning and woodwork admiringly, while she rocked, dreamed and pretended to her heart's content. Lately it had become the one place where she felt she could be herself, where she could really be free.

"Bueno, we have to go. It's late."

"That's right, me too."

"Wait," Casto told them, "I'll drive you people home."

"You don't have to . . ." Don Isidro protested. "We know you are tired."

"No, I'm not. Besides, I gotta drive ma and Purencia home anyway."

"That's right," Purencia said, "my old man doesn't like me going out at night. It's only because of Mami that he let me. So, Casto has to take me home."

"I gotta get you the chair, wait," Casto said. "And, you don't wanna carry that all the way home. It's not very big, but still, it's a lot to lug around."

"All right then, very good."

Everyone got up and Zoraida began to clear away the dishes.

"Let me help you," Doña Clara said as she stood up.

"Me too," Doña Elvira said, without rising.

"No, no thanks. That's all right. I can do it myself," Zoraida said. "Besides, I have to put the kids to bed and give them their milk and all."

"I don't know how she does it. Three little ones and this place is always immaculate." Doña Clara turned to Doña Elvira. "It's really too much for her, and she has no help at all."

Doña Elvira stood. "She keeps a very clean house," she said and walked out with Purencia following after Casto and Don Isidro.

Doña Clara looked at her daughter, who worked silently and efficiently. "Mira, mi hija, I better talk to you." She stood close to Zoraida and began to speak in a friendly manner keeping her voice low. "You have to humor men; you must know that by now. After all, you are no longer a little girl. All women go through this difficulty, eh? You are not the only one. Why, do you know how many times your father wants . . . well, you know, wants it? But I, that is, if I don't want to do it, well I find a way not to. But diplomatically, you know? All right, he's older now and he bothers me less; still, what I mean is, you have to learn that men are like babies and they feel rejected unless you handle the situation just right. Now, we'll take the rocker back home with us because it will make him feel better. But you must do your part too. Tell him you have a headache, or a backache, or you can even pretend to be asleep. However, once in a while you have to please him, you know. After all, he does support you and the children and he needs it to relax. What's the harm in it? It's a small sacrifice. Listen, I'll give you some good advice; make believe you are enjoying it and then get it over with real quick, eh? So, once in a while you have to, whether you like it or not; that's just the way it is for us. Okay? Do you understand?" Zoraida turned away and, without responding, continued with her work. "Did you hear what I just told you?" Doña Clara grabbed Zoraida's shoulder firmly, squeezing her fingers against the flesh. "You didn't even hear what I said to you!"

Zoraida pulled away and turned quickly facing her mother.

She looked directly at Doña Clara, "I heard you . . ." Zoraida stopped and a smile passed her lips. "I heard every word you said, Mami."

"Oh, all right then . . ." Doña Clara said, somewhat startled by her daughter's smile. "I only wanted to . . ."

"Mama! Come on, it's time to go," Don Isidro's voice interrupted her.

Doña Clara and Zoraida went into the living room. Casto carried the rocking chair and waited by the door. The children had come out of their room and were happily jumping about.

"Look, Mommy, Granpa gave me a quarter," Clarita said.

"Me too," said Eddie. "He even gave Junior one."

"All right, get to bed!" Casto shouted. "Zoraida, put them down, will you?"

Everybody said goodbye and, in a moment, Casto and the others left.

"Mommy, where is Daddy taking your chair?" Clarita asked.

"To Nana's."

"Why?"

"Because they want it now?"

"Don't you want it no more?"

"I already had it for a long time, now they need to have it for a while."

Zoraida gave the children their milk, bathed them and put them to bed. Then, she finished rapidly in the kitchen and went to bed herself. She looked over at the empty space near the window. It was gone. She wouldn't be able to sit there anymore and meet all her suitors and be beautiful. The last time . . . the last time she was dancing to a very slow number, a ballad. But she couldn't remember the words. And she was with, with . . . which one? She just couldn't remember him anymore. If she had the rocker, she could remember; it would all come back to her as soon as she sat down. In fact, she was always able to pick up exactly where she had left off the time before. She shut her eyes, deciding not to think about the rocker, about Casto, Doña Digna or her mother. Instead, Zoraida remembered her children who were safe and asleep in their own beds. In a short while, she heard the front door open and recognized Casto's footsteps. She shut her eyes, turned over, facing away from his side of the bed. Casto found the apartment silent and dark, except for the night light.

In the bedroom, Casto looked at Zoraida, who seemed fast asleep, then at the empty space near the window where the rocker usually stood. Their bedroom seemed larger and his burden lighter. Casto sighed, feeling better. He reached over and lightly touched Zoraida; this was a safe time of the month, maybe she would wake up. He waited and, after a moment, decided to go to sleep. After all, he could always try again tomorrow.

A Time with a Future
(Carmela)

A Time with a Future
(Carmela)

"A whole lifetime together, imagine! And now it's over."
Edna spoke, holding back tears. "I don't know what I would do
if I were Mama, honest."

"Poor Mama," murmured Mary, "she's had such a hard time
of it. I'm glad that in these last few years they had each other.
Papa was her whole life . . ." Mary stopped and began to sob
quietly. Edna put her arms around Mary, who buried her head in
her sister's bosom. "Oh Edna, it's so sad to see it all come to an
end. The end of something so special."

"Come on, Mary." Edna very gently pushed Mary away from
her. "Let's not get like this. Think of Ma. If she sees us crying,
it'll be worse for her. We all have to figure this thing out calmly
and rationally."

"I know." Mary wiped her eyes and swallowed. "It's . . . the
finality of it that's so hard for me to bear, you know? But you're
right, we're all Mom's got now, so it's up to us to decide what's
best. At her age, it's like you say, she can't be left alone."

"That's more like it, and we can't stay here day after day
indefinitely like this. I don't know how long Joe's mother is
going to hold out with my kids. How about you? Exactly how
long do you think Mark's gonna come home from work to take
care of your three and do housework? That's why, when Roberto

gets here, I'll discuss what Joe and I have agreed to. Then all three of us have to sit down and decide Mama's future."

Carmela had left her daughters seated in the kitchen, entered the small bedroom of her four-room flat and closed the door, shutting out their voices. She was sick of her daughters' tear-stained faces, their wailing, crying and self-pity. Grown women, with families, acting like children. Carmela shook her head; it was all too much. Her whole body was tired; every bone, every muscle ached. She pulled back the bedspread, kicked off her shoes and lay down.

They had buried Benjamin two days ago, but her daughters had insisted on remaining with her both nights. And that meant Carmela had to make the daybed in the other room, share her own bed with one of her daughters, find more sheets, towels, dishes and all the extra work that was part of caring for others. She had not been able to rest; not as she should, by herself, alone with her private grief and deep sense of relief. There had been too many people at the funeral. Benjamin's friends from the union, neighbors and people she had not seen in years. Carmela felt her eyelids closing with a heaviness from lack of sleep. She had not really slept peacefully in over a week and, before that, for what had seemed like a timeless battle, she had hardly known sleep at all.

Her mind was still filled with him, with Benjamin. When they had laid Benjamin out in the casket, they had pinned a bright scarlet carnation on the lapel of his best suit. The rich red color of the flower contrasted sharply with the dry greyness of his skin and accentuated the dark purple lines of pain that the long illness had etched in his face. Carmela had asked the morticians to replace the red carnation with a white one; this change had made it easier to look at him.

She remembered her Freddie all too vividly. There are things one never forgets, always feels. Like my Freddie, Carmela nodded. His small casket had been laden with flowers. They had placed a bright red rose in his hands which were cupped together as if in prayer. For him, this had been the right color, matching his full red mouth which was fixed in a serene smile. He appeared to be sleeping and, for one long moment, Carmela had actually believed that Freddie would look up, his dark eyes smiling, and question her. "Where am I, Mami? What am I doing here?" And she would respond, "A bad dream, my baby. Freddie, you and me, we are both having a bad dream."

But it was no dream. Freddie's illness had been unexpected, swift and real. In a matter of days she had lost him. Not like Benjamin; more than a year of waiting patiently for him to die.

At first it had seemed no more than a bad cold. Freddie had a low fever and a sore throat. But he got sicker and his breathing became difficult, then unbearable. With each intake of air, he emitted a rasping, honking sound, and his small chest caved in, then extended until it seemed about to burst. Carmela was frightened and alone. Benjamin was on the night shift again. While the others slept soundly, Carmela dressed Freddie warmly. She went to a neighbor and asked her to look after the children until she returned from the clinic with Freddie. The bus was not there, and Carmela decided it would be quicker to walk the many long blocks to the emergency clinic. Even through the blankets she could feel Freddie struggling to breathe as she carried him as fast as her feet could take her. At the emergency clinic she explained with great effort in her halting English why she was there, and then waited for her name to be called.

The young doctor spoke gently to her. "You have a very sick baby. He must stay here, in the hospital. Understand . . . mother? Usted comprende? Si, very good." Carmela's head was spinning. She asked "But how? Why? He all right yesterday. He play with the brother and sisters. Por favor, doctor, give to me the medicina, and I take care of my baby in home. Mi casa is much better for him, yes?" The young doctor shook his head, "No! He's too sick to leave hospital." Lifting his hands, he covered his head and face, gesturing to her. "We have to put him in an oxygen tent so he can breathe. He has pneumonia, under-

stand? Muy enfermo niño . . . comprende, madre?" She felt
the fear deep inside, shivering as if someone had replaced her
blood with ice water. "Por favor, doctor, he never go away from
me, he no talk good English too much . . . pero Freddie under-
stands good everything. He no go in school . . . only cuatro,
four years." The young doctor nodded reassuringly, "He'll be
all right in hospital, Mrs. Puig, you go home to your casa. Take
care of your other children. Then you can came back later and
stay with Freddie. The nurse will give you all the information.
Don't worry, no apures, we are going to take good care of your
baby. Make him well. Go home, get some rest." As they took
him away, Freddie had turned to her, wide-eyed and scared,
fighting for breath.

As soon as Benjamin came home from work, Carmela
returned, staying by Freddie's side for the better part of two
days. Freddie was not improving, but he had not gotten worse.
When he was awake, he smiled at her from under the oxygen tent
and she smiled back, telling him all about the things she would
get for him after he got well again.

When on the third day she had made her brief visit home to
check on the others, Benjamin complained.

"Two days! Two days! I can't stay out another day. Woman,
what am I gonna do for money to buy food, pay rent . . . when
they dock me? I must get back to work. Freddie's all right now.
He's in the best place, in the hospital with the doctors who know
better than you what to do." This time Carmela fought back.
"But if something should happen to him, I want to be there at his
side. Freddie mustn't be alone." Benjamin was unshaken. "I
can't be here with the kids, cooking, washing and doing your
housework . . . just in case something happens! There's plenty
men out there looking for jobs. I'll lose my job . . . woman! If
you want to go when I'm not here, call in a neighbor or get a
friend. How about Sara, you've done her plenty of favors, eh?"
Carmela resisted. "What friends? When do I have time to make
friends? Neighbors can't be staying here all day with our kids,

and neither can Sara. Besides, she's alone with her own children and worse off than us. There's only you; nobody else can stay here except you. Ben . . . maybe you can ask for part-time work just a few more days until Freddie is over the crisis . . . maybe . . ." Benjamin shouted, "Stop it!" Full of his own fears, his mind raced with memories of his childhood in a time where death and starvation had dictated his existence. And for two days now, the words to a song he had not heard since he was a small boy would not leave his mind; they played on his lips over and over.

First the tremors,
then the typhoid
follows hunger with every breath
we pray for joy, for better times
but the only relief is the promise of death!

The peasants of his tiny rural village would sing this song during the typhoid epidemic. Benjamin had lost his father, two older brothers and baby sister, leaving only his mother, older sister and younger brother. He was nine when he became head of the household. Sometimes he would get work at the fields or at the sugar refinery, working from sun-up to sundown, bringing home twenty-five, maybe thirty cents a day, depending on the work to be done. Other days he would work chopping wood, running errands and cleaning the hog pens, to be paid in food; usually leftovers, but enough so that they wouldn't starve at home. At thirteen, when his mother died, his sister found work as a domestic and he and his younger brother set out on their own.

"Absolutely not, woman! There's a goddam depression out there. Do you think I'm gonna let us all starve? I ain't selling apples or shoelaces in the street, not when I got a job to go to. And we don't take charity in this family. I go back to work

tomorrow and you . . . you can do what the hell you want!"
Carmela kept silent. Benjamin had a strong will and his fears
justified his reasoning. She understood she could not persuade
him.

Carmela had not wanted Freddie to die alone in the hospital,
but that's how it had happened. For the next three days, she had
only been able to be with him for a few hours, and always with
the thought of the others that she left at home, unattended for the
most part. That evening when Mr. Cooper, owner of the candy
store, sent a message that the hospital had called on the public
phone asking her to come right away, Carmela guessed what it
was they would tell her.

"Too late. We did everything we possibly could." The young
doctor was compassionate and visibly upset. "Double pneumonia . . . there was nothing we could give him. All of us did the
best we could. We are all very, very sorry. Mrs. Puig, Freddie
was a wonderful little boy."

That was in another lifetime, the time of the Great Depression, before the Second World War, before penicillin, antibiotics
and miracle drugs. Today it would have been different; children
don't have to die from that illness anymore. Medicine, in this
lifetime, knows no limits. Look at an old man like Benjamin,
eh? Kept alive, full of disease and tortured by pain beyond
human endurance. And for what? No future, no hope, only the
knowledge that each day he remained alive would be a torment
for both of them.

Carmela opened her eyes and yawned, stretching her body.
There was no sense in expecting sleep to come, take over and
soothe away her weariness. Too much was still happening
inside, repeating itself. The past was still the present and the
present was not yet real.

When the doctor told her about Benjamin, she had insisted he
be told as well. It was too much for her at this time; no longer did
she have that kind of strength for others. Besides, Benjamin was
a proud man, and it was only right. He had already suspected

what the doctors confirmed; he was frightened, but not shocked. Calmly, Benjamin had told her he was resigned to the inevitable, but wanted to ask her for one last favor. And that request stirred and brought to the surface those deep and private feelings of hatred and revenge that can only be felt by one human being for another when they have been as close as Benjamin and Carmela. Then, as he spoke, Carmela felt herself spinning with rage.

"Carmela, no matter how sick I get, don't send me away. Let me die here in my own bed, Carmelita, here with you, by your side."

A tirade of words she had been nurturing, rehearsing and storing away for that day when she would leave him, walk out, walk out for good, choked Carmela. "Remember Freddie? Remember our son, Benjamin? How he died alone? In a strange place, in a strange bed. Without me by his side. I owed him at least as much as you ask of me. A baby, four years old with no one to comfort him from the fear of death, to guide him gently into the unknown. It all happened thirty-eight years ago, but I remember. And now, today, now . . . you want the right to die here, safe and secure in my arms. I didn't give birth to you! You selfish, hateful man, how well I know you!"

They had looked at each other silently. He, waiting for her to answer. She, unable to speak, afraid of that explosion of terrible words that would vent her rage. Now it was so easy to hurt him, to make him suffer as she had suffered the death and loss of her child. She couldn't speak, not one word left her lips. Carmela saw him old and tired, bracing himself against death, preparing himself and seeking her help. He spoke again, this time pleading.

"Promise, Carmela, that's all I ask of you. Just this favor and never will I ask you for another thing; I give you my word . . . just don't, don't send me away; no matter what, let me die at home."

Carmela had hidden her resentment and put aside her hatred. Instead, she responded as always, to the unspoken bond that existed between them, that dependency on each other.

And she had promised, "It'll be all right, Benjamin, you can remain at home. No matter how sick you get. Don't worry, I won't let them take you away. You can stay here with me . . . until it's over."

This pact, built on survival, was what held them together; it was what had cemented them to a lifetime of sharing without so much as a day's voluntary separation. That security, that dependency, was the foundation of their marriage; solid and tough, like a boulder of impenetrable granite.

For a full year she had nursed him, giving him medicine, caring for him as he got weaker, almost every minute of the day and night. In time, she had to bathe him, give him the bedpan and finally spoon-feed him. His body, at first, was still strong and straight. They had not slept together for many years and so Carmela had been amazed by his supple body, the muscular limbs and tightness of skin that was unusual for a man as old as Benjamin. But, as he got sicker and lost weight, his body became frail and bent; his skin hung loosely as if lightly tacked onto his bones.

The sleepless nights, when he called out to her for comfort not once, but constantly . . . the three flights she had to climb, loaded with bundles, began to rip Carmela apart. The burden of his illness gave her no time to rest. Completely exhausted, she decided to speak to him about her promise.

"Benjamin, maybe it's better for you in the hospital. Listen, think about it, please. They can care for you better there, give you stronger medicine, maybe, eh? Look, Benjamin, I'm so tired, because there's nothing more I can do for you. Please, I don't know how long I can hold out . . . please think about it. I promise, I'll be out to see you every day; every single day I'll be by your side at the hospital, I swear . . ."

"No, you promised me! And now you talk about sending me out! You said I could stay. Carmela, you've become hard-hearted to say this to me. No!" His eyes had filled with tears.

Like a child, he clung desperately to her, grabbing her hands, groping at her body. "Please, in the name of God . . . please don't send me away. Let me die here, with you . . . you promised!" Carmela had pushed him away, tearing at his fingers, shoving and struggling, unable to free herself from his fierce grip. "You promised! Now that I'm dying, I don't matter anymore . . . you can't send me away . . . you can't . . ."

"Selfish man, you deserve to die alone, just like my dead baby! It would be justice to send you away . . . away from me."

Again the words remained unspoken; instead, she said "All right, stop it! Stop! For God's sake, you can stay, I promise you. But I'm getting some help. I can't do it all alone. All right, I said you can stay!" Only then, after she had reassured him, had Benjamin released her.

Carmela had run away to the other side of the apartment and had put her hands over her ears to shut out his crying. But she still heard his loud sobbing and screaming.

"Carmela, Carmelita, you are a good woman!"

Carmela was able to get some help; a practical nurse came three times a week and later, every day. Benjamin journeyed each day on a long painful road that would lead to death. The kind of merciless journey that comes with cancer. The cancer had started in his lower intestines and finally ran rampant through his body, leaving him helpless, barely able to move. But still he clung to life, determined to put up a battle; fighting to survive was all he knew.

He would call out "Carmela . . . get me some water, Carmela, I don't want the nurse, tell her to leave. Do something for this pain! Carmela, give me something. Don't leave me, Carmela." And she would hope and pray that before he could utter her name once more, he would stop breathing.

Then, at last, he lapsed into a coma, feebly clinging to life. He would utter sounds and sentences which were, for the most part, unintelligible. Sometimes he screamed out the names of his own parents, brothers and sisters. Events of his childhood, memories of back home filled his mind and escaped from his lips. He spoke mostly in Spanish, laughing, crying and asking questions. No one knew what he wanted and, after two days, no one listened except Carmela. Maybe at this time, Carmela hoped, he would say something about their dead child; but in all his tangled words and gibberish, Freddie's name was never mentioned.

Her children had been at the apartment since their father's latest turn for the worse. That day, they all sat in the kitchen, drinking coffee and hot chocolate, waiting for him to die. They shared the vigil, taking turns at Benjamin's bedside. Late that evening, Roberto called his mother and when she returned, they found Benjamin staring blankly, not breathing. A look of peace spread over his face, as if the pain had finally disappeared. Gently, Carmela closed his eyes and mouth, kissed his dry lips and covered his face with the sheet.

Again, thoughts about the funeral, the people, the flowers and Freddie crowded Carmela's thoughts. It was as if her thinking pattern were following a cycle, winding up always with Benjamin's death.

Perhaps she was avoiding this latest part of the whole business? Carmela knew she had to deal with her children, grownups who still insisted on that relationship of mother and child. Now they felt themselves to be in charge, Carmela sighed, almost out of patience. She heard the front door and voices. That would be Roberto, and now her children would begin another discussion about her future.

She had been through their weddings, the birth of their children, marital disputes from time to time; always she had listened and given her support. What they wanted now, and what they might ask of her, created an anxiety that drained Carmela's energy. In a few minutes she would get up and speak to them. Sooner or later they had to talk.

"Mama can come home with me, we'll find the room; Suzie and Gigi can double up . . ." Mary looked at her brother and sister nervously, then continued, "Mark won't mind, honest."

"No," Edna responded, "I think it's better if she comes with me; after all, we have the big house. Nobody will be put out for space."

"I wish I could say it's all right at my house, but the way things are with me and Gloria, well . . ." Roberto hesitated.

"We understand, don't worry," Edna said. "Besides, it's better for Mama to be with her own daughter."

"Financially, I can always help out, you know that," Roberto smiled.

"She's got Papa's pension and some savings; she's all right as far as that goes," Edna said, "but if we need anything more, I'll let you know."

"There's only one thing about her going with you," Mary said. "She's not gonna want to go way out to Long Island. Port Jefferson is too far away from everything for her."

"She'll get used to it. It'll take a little time, that's all. Anyway, you're far away yourself, Mary. Mount Vernon isn't around the corner! And your apartment isn't big enough for another person. Where are you gonna put her?"

"You know what I think? I don't think we are gonna get Mama out of this old apartment, period." Roberto nodded emphatically. "She's too attached to it. Remember the time they took a trip to Puerto Rico, back to Papa's town, to see about retiring there? Ma said she couldn't stand it. She missed the city, her friends, everything. How long have they been living here in this place? Twenty-six years or something like that, right?"

"It'll be better for her to leave here. Personally, I don't know how anybody can live here, in this city, if they can get out . . ." Edna shook her head, "The noise, the pollution, the crime! Oh, I know I wouldn't want my kids here. When we were kids, maybe it was different . . . it just seems worse today . . ."

"Mama said it's not too bad since they put up all the new middle-income buildings. She says it's better than ever with new shops and all kinds of interesting people around. Ma says she can go right to Broadway and buy anything she wants at any time of the day or . . ."

"Stop being so naive . . ." Edna interrupted. "Mary, how long can Mama stay by herself? She's sixty-six. In a few years, when she can't cope, then what? It'll be a lot worse to get her out of here. I'm not going to be commuting back and forth. And I know you, Mary . . . you too, Roberto, especially the way your marriage is going, who knows where you'll be, eh? No, we have to make a decision between us and stick to it. Now, listen to what Joe and I have planned . . ." Edna paused, making sure her brother and sister were listening. "Mama has a fairly good income from Papa's pension, so she won't be a financial burden to anyone. She's in good health, except for some arthritis now and then, but nobody ever hears her complain. And, she has some savings . . . all right, then. With a little more than half her savings we can convert the playroom area on the lower level of my house into living quarters for Mama. Like a kind of efficiency apartment, with her own kitchenette and half-bath. She won't need much more because she will have the rest of the house as well. This is necessary because we all know how independent Mama is. After that initial investment, I won't charge her rent or anything. She can live there as long as she wants . . . I mean, for the rest of her days."

Roberto opened his mouth to speak, but thought better of it. Instead, he shrugged and smiled, looking at Mary. She smiled back. After a long silence, Mary said, "It sounds pretty good . . . what do you think, Roberto?" "Well, so far it's the best plan, and also the only plan. There's only one thing, like I said, Ma's gotta go for it." "She will," Edna said, "but it's up to us to convince her. The two of you better back me on this. Understand? We have to be united in this thing? Well?" Mary and Roberto nodded in agreement. "Good," Edna continued, "now, what to do with this place? Mama's got all kinds of pots and pans . . . look at all of this furniture and junk. I suppose she'll want to take some of this with her . . . let's see . . . "

Carmela sat up, put on her shoes and placed the bedspread

neatly back on her bed. She heard the voices of her children. Well, she might as well get it over with. Carmela opened a bureau drawer, removed a small grey metal box and opened it. She searched among her valuable papers; the will she and Benjamin had made, the life insurance policy she had taken out on herself many years ago and still faithfully paid every month, some very old photographs, letters from her children as youngsters and from her grandchildren. Finally, she found the large manilla envelope with all the material she was looking for. She closed the box and put it back. Then she walked into the kitchen where her children were waiting.

"Ma, how you feeling?" Roberto kissed his mother lightly on the forehead.

"How about something to eat, Ma?" Edna asked. "Some tea? Or a little hot broth?"

"No," Carmela sat, holding the envelope in her hands. "I'm fine; I'm not hungry."

"Mama, you should eat more, you're getting too thin . . . it's not good for you. You should eat regularly, it could affect your . . ."

"Ma . . ." interrupted Edna, ignoring Mary, "we have to have a serious talk."

"I wasn't finished," snapped Mary.

"Mama's not hungry!" Edna looked directly at Mary. "All right?"

"Listen . . ." Roberto spoke. "Why don't I go out and get us all something to eat. Chinese or Cuban . . . so nobody has to cook."

"Sit down, Roberto." Edna then continued in a quiet, calm voice, "We have all the food we need here . . ." Turning to Carmela, she went on, "Mama, now that Papa isn't here anymore . . . we want you to know that you have us and you don't have to be alone. You are our responsibility now, just as if you had Papa. We all know this . . . don't we?" She turned to Mary and Roberto.

"Yes."

"Oh yes, Mama."

"We've all discussed this a great deal, just between ourselves. And, we've decided on a plan that we know you'll like. Of course, we want to talk it over with you first, so that we have your approval. But, I'm certain that when you hear what it is, you'll be pleased."

"Oh yes, Mama, wait until you hear what Edna . . . what we . . . oh, go ahead, Edna, tell her . . ." Mary smiled.

"Joe and I agreed and thought this out carefully. You . . . are coming to live with us, Mama. With me, Joe and the kids. We are the ones with a big house. Mary's in an apartment and Roberto doesn't exactly know where he's gonna settle; not the way things are right now. I know how proud you are and how independent, so you'll want to contribute something. Here's what we think . . . you know my house is a split level and there's room for expansion, right?"

Carmela felt an urge to open the envelope at that moment and tell them, so that Edna could stop talking nonsense. But instead, she listened, trying to hide her impatience.

". . . so that your savings, or part anyway, can pay for your private apartment. Of course, as I said, you don't need such a big area, because you can share the house with the rest of us. Outside, you can take a section of the lot, Mama, if you want to have a vegetable garden or flowers. The kids would love it, and of course Joe and I won't take a cent, you can live the rest of your days rent free. You know Joe's pleased, he wants you to feel welcomed in our home." Edna was almost out of breath. "Well, there, I've said my piece . . . now what do you think, Mama?"

All three waited for Carmela to respond. She held out the envelope.

"I've got something to show all of you." Carefully she removed its contents and spread several sheets of paper out on the kitchen table. "I suppose I should have said something before this, but with your father's illness and everything else . . ." Carmela gestured that they come closer. "Here we are . . . take a look. It's a co-op. The building's only been up about three years. Everything is brand new. My apartment is on the sixteenth floor, on the northwest corner, just like I wanted, with lots of windows and it's got a terrace! Imagine, a terrace . . . I'm gonna feel rich . . . that's what. Look . . . kids, here are the floor plans, see? I got one bedroom, a living room-dining room, a brand-new kitchen. Oh, and here's an incinerator for garbage. They've got one on every floor and a community room with all kinds of activities. I heard from some of the people who live there, that there are some well-known experts, lecturers, coming in to speak about all kinds of subjects. The best part is that it's right here, around the corner, on Amsterdam Avenue. On the premises we have a drugstore, stationery and delicatessen. You know, I put my name down for this with a deposit right after Papa got sick. He hadn't wanted us to move, but once I knew how things would be, I went ahead. They called me just before Benjamin died, when he was almost in a coma, and asked if I could move in around the first of the month. I took a chance . . . I knew he couldn't last much longer, and said yes. That's in two weeks!" Carmela was busy tracing the floor plans with her fingers showing them the closets and cabinet space. "Here? See, I've paid the purchase, my savings covered the amount. You are all welcome to come and sit on the terrace . . . wait until you see how beautiful it is . . ."

"Mama . . ." Edna's voice was sharp, "what about what I just said? I finished explaining to you . . . a very important plan concerning your future. What about it?"

"I'm moving the first of the month, Edna," Carmela continued to look at floor plans. "But, I thank you and your husband for thinking of me."

"Is that it, Mama?"

"Yes, Edna."

"You already signed the lease, paid the money and everything?"

"Yes, all I have to do is move in, Edna."

"Well . . . I'm glad to see you figured it all out, Mama." Edna looked at Mary and Roberto; they avoided her eyes. "There's just one thing, eh? Who is gonna look after you when you can't . . . ?" You are sixty-six, ma! Sixty-six!"

"Not you, Edna." Carmela looked at her children. "Or you, Mary, or you, Roberto."

"Mama, I don't think you are being practical. Now, I'm too far away to be here if anything happens! If you get sick . . . and so is Mary. And as far as Roberto is concerned . . ."

"I'll manage."

"Manage? Please, Mama. Mary, Roberto, what do you have to say? Don't you think Mama should have asked us first about this? Mama, you should have spoken to us! After all, we are your children."

"I didn't ask any of you to come here when Papa was so sick, did I? I never called or bothered you. I took care of all of you once, and I took care of him . . . now, I want the privilege of taking care of myself!" There was a long silence and Carmela continued. "Thank you Edna, Mary, Roberto; you are all good children. But I can take care of myself; I've done it all my life."

"If that's the way you see it, Mama, I'm with you." Roberto said. "Right, Mary?"

"Okay . . . I guess . . ." Mary smiled weakly at Edna.

"All right, Mama." Edna stood up. "Go ahead . . . but remember, I tried my best to work something out for you. When something happens, you won't have anybody near you."

"I appreciate your good intentions, Edna, but it's all settled."

"When are you moving in, Mama?" asked Mary.

"I hope on the first, but since the landlord here knows me so well after twenty-six years, and we always paid our rent, I might be able to stay a few days extra, if things are not ready at the new place. I've already arranged everything with the movers and with the super of the new building and . . ."

They spoke for a while and Carmela talked excitedly about

her new apartment.

"I feel better now that you all know . . . in fact," a feeling of drowziness overcame her, "I think I might take a nap."

"Mama," Edna said, "we are all gonna have to leave soon, you know, get back to our families. But if you need us, please call."

"Good," Carmela smiled, "we should all get back to our own business of living, eh? The dead are at peace, after all. You were all a great help. Your husbands and children need you, and you too, Roberto . . . Gloria and the kids would like to see you, I'm sure."

"Go on, Mama, take your nap. Edna and I will cook something light, and then I think I'll call Mark to pick me up."

Carmela put everything back into her envelope and left. She closed her door and lay down, a sweet twilight state embraced her; it seemed to promise a deep sleep.

"Papa isn't even buried more than two days and she's acting like he's been dead forever." Edna was on the verge of tears. "She looks so happy . . . I don't understand it. You would think . . . Oh, I don't know anymore!"

"I'm sure she feels bad," Mary said, "it's just that she's also happy about her new apartment."

"She feels bad, all right. Mama doesn't want to show it, so that we don't feel worse than we already do," Roberto said.

"Well then, why is it that when Papa died she hardly cried. A few tears and moist eyes, but you can't call that crying.!"

"Well, what do you want from her?" Roberto snapped.

"I don't know! She should be sorry . . . yes, that's what; I want her to be sorry!"

"What do you mean, sorry?!" Roberto whispered angrily.

"He was her husband of a lifetime, and my father, I . . ." Edna's voice became louder "want her to feel it!"

"Shh . . ." Mary snapped, "stop it!"

"How do you know what she feels inside? Leave her alone! It's always what you want? What about what she wants?"

"Go on, defend her. You've always been her favorite; mama's boy!"

"Quit that shit!" Roberto went towards Edna.

"For God's sake," Mary whimpered, "we're acting like kids . . . what's happening?"

"That's right, whimper like a baby, Mary." Edna began to cry, "that's all you know how to do. Everybody else has to make your decisions . . ."

"This is ridiculous," Roberto said, "I'm leaving."

"Go on . . . walk out, that's what you always do, you've done it to your own family now."

"Screw you . . . bitch!" Roberto called out, then slammed the front door.

"Come on, Edna, please stop it. What's the use of fighting? Mama's made up her mind. Let's make supper and forget about all of this. Roberto will come back after he cools off. You better call Joe; I think it's time we went home."

The two sisters began to open the refrigerator and pantry to prepare the evening meal. Mary turned to Edna, who was still sobbing quietly.

"What's the matter now?"

"I . . . wish she would be sorry . . ."

Carmela stood on the small terrace of her new apartment. She looked down at the city laid out before here. In between and over some of the buildings she could see the Hudson River and part of the George Washington Bridge. The river was dotted with sailboats and small craft that slipped in and out of sight. Overhead she had a view of a wide blue sky, changing clouds competing with the bright sun. Flocks of birds were returning home now that winter was over. Carmela took a deep breath. There was a warmth in the air; spring was almost here. In a couple of weeks she could bring out her new folding chair, lounger and snack table. Soon she would bring out her plants. New buds would begin to sprout, growing strong and healthy with the abundant sunlight and fresh air.

Carmela missed no one in particular. From time to time her children and grandchildren visited. She was pleased to see them for a short while and then was even happier when they left. In a few days it would be a whole year since Benjamin's death. It seemed like yesterday sometimes, and sometimes it was like it never happened.

She rarely thought about Benjamin. Memories of her days as a young girl became frequent, clear and at times quite vivid. Before Carmela had married at sixteen, she had dreamed of traveling to all the many places she had seen in her geography book. After school she would often go with her brothers to the docks of San Juan just to watch the freightors and big ships.

"When I grow up I'm going to work and travel on those ships." "Carmelita, don't be silly, you can't. Girls can't join the navy or the merchant marine."

How she had wished she had been born a boy, to be able to travel anywhere, to be part of that world. Carmela loved the water; ocean, sea, river, all gave her a feeling of freedom.

She looked out from her terrace at the river, and a sense of peace filled her whole being. Carmela recognized it was the same exhilarating happiness she had experienced as a young girl, when each day would be a day for her to reckon with, all her own, a time with a future.

Brief Miracle
(Virginia)

Brief Miracle
(Virginia)

"It's a miracle, what's happened to them two since they been together."

"These things are meant to be. Fate works like that . . . me, I'm a believer in fate."

The two men sat at the bar discussing the couple seated at a table at the far end of the room.

"The best thing is the way Virginia provides a home for Mateo and his kids . . . better than their own mother. Bunny never cared for them like she does. They were always neglected, dirty, hungry. And . . . I heard she used to leave them alone . . . to run around."

"Well, but Bunny was only fourteen when she started having kids, right? And then, she didn't stop; they kept on having so many . . . like rabbits! In a way, who could blame her? The problem was she was just a kid herself."

"No matter . . . I say motherhood is sacred. I mean, you're the father. Anybody can be a father . . . it's being the mother that means a special responsibility. That's nature, the way God made things. If a woman can't care for kids, then don't go giving birth. That's what I say!"

"You got a point there, friend. I know, because with my old lady, the kids are always first. I can't get her to go out sometimes . . . and you know why? She don't wanna leave the children alone . . . not even with a sitter. Nobody can care for them like her, she says. Now, I got me a good wife and mother for my kids."

"The day I get hooked, man, I hope I get me an old lady as fine as yours. Let's drink to her."

"And, to her." They both looked at the attractive woman seated with the man. "She's good people. Whatever she done before, she's made up for it now." They lifted their drinks.

"A toast to . . . motherhood!"

"Para todas las madres . . . right on, bro!"

Virginia and Mateo had been introduced at this very tavern, less than four months ago. Since then, they had set up house together. This fact, in itself, was not all that unusual. Ordinarily, no one would have paid them much attention, but it was who they were and why they had gotten together that caused people to talk.

Ten years ago Mateo had been forced to marry his pregnant fourteen-year-old sweetheart. Five more children had been born in eight years. Despite his chronic drinking, he had held on to a steady job all these years in order to support his family. Things had become worse for him when two years ago, Bunny, his wife, had left him. She took the three oldest children and their infant, leaving Mateo with the two younger, middle children. With the help of his sick mother, Mateo had managed to keep his two children, parenting them as best he could. Everyone commented on what a shame it was that a man not yet thirty could let himself look like a derelict; rarely sober, always in need of clean clothes, a shave and a bath. But it was also amazing, they had to admit, that in his condition, Mateo could still keep his job. As a friend had said, Mateo's life was one of "aimless survival."

Virgina had quit school and run away from home ten years ago, when she had just turned sixteen. Her story, as far as people knew, was as follows. Virginia had been seduced by and had fallen in love with her English teacher, an attractive woman in her middle thirties. The affair had gone on undetected, until Virginia's parents found love letters exchanged by the teacher and their daughter. They threatened to press charges and planned to

send Virginia to a convent school. That was when the two of
them disappeared, and no one knew to where. There was not
even a note nor hint to her parents. After almost a year of inquiries and following false leads in trying to trace the English
teacher and their daughter, and after exhausting all possibilities
as to where either one might be, Virginia's parents had given up
the search.

When, after all these years, Virginia appeared one evening at
Rickey's Tavern, people barely recognized her. She had developed into a very handsome, elegant woman; well-dressed, very
feminine, not at all what people had imagined. No one dared ask
her about the teacher nor attempted to bring up that incident of
ten years ago. Everyone had been impressed with her confident
manner and the relaxed way she had of talking.

"What have I done? Let's see . . . what haven't I done!
Office work, slinging hash, selling, even producing cosmetics at
home for a while. Finally, I got into textile designing; that's my
specialty now . . . it's not something anyone can do, it's a real
skill. I've always had a talent for drawing and art, so when I was
working as a clerk at this textile plant, the opportunity presented
itself, and I . . ."

Virginia had been reacquainting herself with several persons
at the bar whom she had not seen in more than a decade. Mateo
had been standing a few feet away from the group. He found himself listening and staring at Virginia. She looked somehow
familiar, but he couldn't quite place her. She returned his gaze,
smiling, and began to direct much of what she said to him.
Slowly he inched his way into the group.

"Hey Mat, remember Virginia, don't you? Virginia Solar
from over on Washington Avenue." Someone introduced them.
Mateo nodded, but actually he didn't remember her at all.

After the others had left, Virginia and Mateo continued their
conversation. They found lots to talk about. At first it was Mateo
who asked questions, curious about someone who had been
away for so many years. Mateo had never left the neighborhood,

and Virginia seemed to him a world traveler. Mateo had held that one job at the plant since he was nineteen. Virginia had managed a vast assortment of jobs.

"It must be great to travel and be free like that. You know, see all kinds of things, meet different people. I'll bet you got some interesting stories to tell."

"Sometimes it was interesting . . . but, on the other hand, it must also be a good feeling to know you got a steady home with people who need you, count on you. That part of life seems very important to me."

"Well, I sure got plenty who count on me." Mateo paused, smiled and shook his head. "In that respect, I guess I'm lucky."

"Hey, I'm not saying it isn't hard on you. I'm sure you haven't got it easy. You said your kids are with your mom? Tell me about them . . . how old are they? Boys, girls or both?"

"Both; a boy six, Sammy. A girl four and a half, Lillie. Bunny, my wife, took four and I kept these two. It's funny, I don't know how she decided who got who, but she did. Dividing the kids was rough . . . I mean, you don't think I want this one and not the other. It's like they all belong together . . . and each kid is part of one unit. And if you take any piece of this unit apart, it won't work no more, you know? Anyway, I'm glad Bunny's the one that done it, because I don't know who I would have picked. As things are now, I don't see the others. She thought it better if we just separated, period. So, we don't see them, and they don't see us. We are totally apart. I send support. What the court ordered and no more! That's it. Recently, I heard she's got some guy living with her and that he helps out. Actually . . ." Mateo shrugged, "the less I know the better. We're making out all right; my kids and me . . . we're hanging in there. Oh, at first it was tough, they missed the others. You see, they were all real close . . . but after some time . . ." Virginia listened, responding with a nod now and then, encouraging him to continue. After a while Mateo realized that he was confiding in this woman, a stranger . . . saying things that he preferred never to mention: his marriage, divorce and painful separation from his children. "Hey, here I am running off at the mouth, like some kind of fool. I hope I ain't boring the shit out of you."

"No! You're definitely not! And you're not a fool either. I asked you about yourself because I want to know. Listen, Mateo," Virginia hesitated, then spoke very gently, "I'm not just interested in anybody, I'm interested in you . . . honest."

"Okay . . . and I'll be honest too. I'm embarrassed to say this . . . but I don't remember you; not at all. I mean, at first you looked a little familiar, and I'm trying to think, but," Mateo shrugged, "sorry."

"You know, I thought so. I knew you didn't remember me. I could tell by your eyes. You've got honest eyes, Mateo. I like that. Well, I'm Frank and Ernestina Solar's daughter . . . ring a bell? No? All right then, I'm the girl who ten years ago ran away with the English teacher over at the high school. The woman English teacher. Now do you remember? Everybody talked about it then. I was famous as the neighborhood . . . queer. You've gotta remember that!"

For a moment Mateo looked perplexed and was unable to answer. They remained silent for a while.

"Oh, yeah, now I remember." He picked up his drink and toasted toward her. "So you didn't live happily ever after, eh? Neither did I, baby; that makes two of us."

Virginia laughed and lifted her glass, accepting his toast. "I'll drink to that."

"You know, you are one fine looking girl, Virginia. Very foxy."

"Not what you would expect . . . after all that talk, right?"

"Wait up there! How do you know what I expect? There's something you should know about me, baby . . . that is, I don't expect nothing. From nobody. Nothing . . . one way or another. I don't care what you done and with who. I just happen to dig you, that's all."

"Okay, I'm sorry. I guess I was off base with you. Truce . . ."

Virginia smiled. They spoke for a while longer, then very slowly Virginia moved closer to him. She checked her wristwatch. "It's still very early. Do you want to go someplace else?"

"Let's go."

They went to a motel and spent most of the night together, and continued to meet there for the next few nights as well. They enjoyed making love, sharing and being intimate. Now they both looked forward to this time when they could be alone together. It was less than a week later, as they sat at Rickey's Tavern, Virginia decided to speak to Mateo.

"Mateo, I want to meet your kids. I feel I want to be more involved in your life, not just sex, but all the rest of it. I want to meet them soon. Listen, I'm tired of running around from place to place. I'm happy since I came back home . . . seeing my folks after all these years. You know that in ten years I maybe sent them three picture cards and a couple of letters . . . and never with a return address. What they must have gone through! Yet, they have accepted me; no questions asked! They just wanted me back. I want to make it up to them . . . and to myself. It's funny, I didn't think I'd be happy here, but I am . . . and I believe it's you . . . really. You, Mateo, have made the difference. What do you say . . . let's try?"

"Virginia, there isn't much I got to offer someone like you. You've been to all kinds of places, seen many different things, and you're used to a whole lot I can't give you."

"That's not so! There is a lot you have to offer. Can't you see? Oh, Mateo, you've already made me happy, given me so much, just this past week. You don't know how much. Much more than some others I've known. Besides, I'm not so perfect. There's something . . . we should talk about . . . you should know . . ."

"Don't," interrupted Mateo, "you don't have to tell me nothing. Virginia, you don't owe me no explanations."

"I know you feel I don't. And you really mean it . . . I can see it in your eyes. That's why I'm so relaxed with you. You don't ask questions. Most people are not like you. They want to know, even when they don't speak outright, you can see it in their faces, that they are wondering and thinking about . . . it." Virginia paused, trying to keep her voice steady. "I do want to talk about it, I want you to know. Sometimes unsaid things can create misunderstandings and, well, it's better if I tell you. In the past . . . they way it's been with me is . . . when I've fallen in love with someone and wanted to be with that someone, it's been the person . . . a man or a woman. It didn't matter to me. It was the person and, I guess, how I felt about that individual. You know, whatever was happening at the time, was what I . . . wanted." Virginia paused. "This isn't easy for me to say, but Mateo, I've known both women and men."

"Do you still, Virginia? I mean, if we're going to be together . . . like this is getting heavy between us . . ." Mateo felt the blood rushing to his face. "I gotta know. Do you still desire women . . . sexually?"

"I desire you, honey, only you. That's what I mean: something else has happened to me, and it's never happened before. You make me understand that I want more out of life than just running from this person to that other person . . . or living in different places. Now I want something steady and real. Mateo . . . someone like you. I want to settle down, raise a family. Can you believe me? Or will what I told you make a difference between us?"

"I believe you, baby. The past is over. What you done is finished. What you do now is what matters with me. Okay?" Mateo reached out and placed his hand on Virginia's. She responded by holding on tightly with both hands. "Frankly, baby, I don't know what a fine looking broad like you sees in a miserable bum like me, eh?"

"Stop it. Mateo, don't put yourself down. You're no bum! You're a good man, loyal to your children. And another thing, I carry my own weight. I'm not broke. I've saved money . . . it's ours. Yes, to use in any way we want. It'll give us a head start."

"You mean that, don't you?"

"Yes."

"Before you meet my kids . . . I want to explain about the situation at my mom's. She's a very sick woman. She has a terrible disease called Parkinsons, also diabetes, and a lot more wrong with her. The kids have been affected by all of this. What you're gonna see, ain't pleasant. It's the best I've been able to do in order to keep going. My mom helps as much as she can . . . but, it's not good."

"Don't worry. It'll be all right. I want to meet them just as soon as I can."

"Just so I told you, that's all, baby."

The following day, Mateo brought Virginia to his home. Despite her self-confidence, Virginia was unprepared for what she saw. Doña Emilia's head bobbed like it was attached to a spring, and her hands shook; she seemed to be in perpetual motion. The small apartment was in a state of disarray, with the shades and curtains drawn, shutting out the daylight. The atmosphere was dark and gloomy. Sammy ran excitedly when he heard their voices, greeting them by shaking his hand and bobbing his head, imitating his grandmother.

"Cut it out, Sammy, before I belt you!" Mateo threatened his son.

In the tiny dark bedroom she shared with her brother, Lillie sat on the bed, sucking her thumb. When she saw them, she turned away facing the wall. Virginia sat next to her and gently touched her shoulder. Lillie jumped forward, shut her eyes and pressed her forehead against the wall.

"I do the best I can, Miss . . ." Doña Emilia had difficulty speaking. "But, as you can see, I've no patience with kids no more. I already raised my own. This is not fair. I told Mateo this is temporary. Bunny's gotta come back and take care of her own, eh? I can't help it if she had so many. I do the best I can, Miss, pero por Dios . . . I'm not well. I'm a sick woman . . . I can barely take care of myself. I got no husband . . ."

After they had left the apartment, Mateo spoke first.

"I warned you . . . and I don't hold you to nothing. It's my problem, not yours."

"Let's get the kids out of there, Mateo . . . the sooner the better, for everyone's sake."

Virginia searched for almost two weeks, inquiring at every apartment building in the neighborhood before she got a lead. It was an old but well-kept, rent-controlled building. The available apartment was large enough for all o f them. Virginia negotiated by bribing the super, buying some of the furniture left by the former tenants at too steep a price, and by securing a three-year lease.

The apartment needed lots of work, and Virginia proved to be quite handy. She worked dilligently all day and long into the night. After his job, Mateo helped, amazed at his new companion's energy and abilities.

"Man, Virginia, you're incredible! You do all this here fixing better than me."

"That's because you don't know how many damned places I've lived in and fixed up. And then, knowing deep down that it wasn't going to last . . . sooner or later I'd split. This is a pleasure, honey, no comparison. After all, this is home, Mateo, home at last!"

They fixed, plastered, painted, and Virginia put up wallpaper. She went to the lumber yard and purchased the wood, making the necessary shelves and even put up a divider in the children's room all by herself.

Her parents were pleased beyond measure. Their two other children, both sons and much older than Virginia, lived far away from them; one was an army career sergeant, and the other had settled in Florida. They had almost given up hope of ever seeing their only daughter. Some sort of miracle had returned Virginia to them, they reasoned, and they were grateful to God for having returned her to them. In time they hoped she would marry, and since Mateo and his wife had not taken their marriage vows in the church, they felt a Catholic ceremony could still be arranged.

"First things first," was how Frank Solar had put it. "She's not sinning this time, not really. Those vicious loudmouths who called her 'queer,' 'maricona' and all those names, now let them choke on their own lies! In time you'll see, Mama, she'll go back to church, receive the Holy Sacrament; everything is going to be . . . right, as it should be."

They gave Virginia and Mateo a brand-new dining room set and insisted on buying clothing for their new "grandchildren."

Virginia had begun to spend more and more time with the children. Much to Doña Emilia's joy, they finally moved out and into their new apartment, leaving her alone — and as she requested, "in peace." It took just a few days for Sammy to adjust. He no longer imitated his grandmother and found it easy to return Virginia's affection. He called her "mommy" almost immediately. Lillie, however, proved a greater challenge. Any attempt to caress or kiss Lillie caused her to strike out and withdraw, not speaking. At first, Virginia thought the little girl might be retarded, but after observing her carefully for a few more days, she decided that Lillie was very frightened. Slowly and with great patience and perseverance, Virginia began to confront Lillie, forcing her to respond. She did this by not reacting to Lillie's tantrums, nor to her whining and gurgling noises which sounded like those of an infant. Instead, Virginia would speak to Lillie in a firm voice, demanding normal behavior. Lillie was made to use a spoon or fork, instead of her fingers, when she ate. She had to wash up and help clear the dishes. In time, this technique began to work. Lillie let Virginia touch her hair, back, even kiss her. At bedtime, Virginia would read to them, then she would move close to Lillie and sing to her. The first time she heard Lillie utter a full sentence was when she joined Virginia in the chorus of her favorite song.

". . . with a knick knack paddy whack, give the dog a bone, this old man came rolling home . . ."

From then on it seemed as if Lillie had always spoken. She chattered on like any average child, asking questions and demanding attention. She even followed Virginia around all day, not wanting to let her new mother out of sight. Sammy attended school and participated in sports and other activities. Mateo bathed and shaved regularly, remaining for the most part sober. He was a shy person by nature, uncommunicative: neither talkative nor inquisitive. After supper, when the kids were bedded down, Mateo and Virginia usually made love. Otherwise, he was content to drink his beer and watch television.

Virginia planned to find part-time work or maybe even bring out her portfolio and try free-lancing as a textile designer. This would be done only after Lillie was registered in school, and Virginia had free time. She loved her new role, shopping, cooking, even fixing the apartment just the way it suited her; Mateo never argued about those things. Virginia looked up old school chums and their families, inviting them for a visit, proudly showing off her new home and family.

However, late at night when everyone was asleep, Virginia would lie awake fighting a sense of fear and apprehension that crept right through her. She kept recalling Cornelia, Sandy, Tim and some of the others she had left behind. Always at the beginning, Virginia had been enthusiastic, determined to make any relationship work. Then, the urgency to leave, get away, reach out for something different became an obsession. She could think of nothing else. When this happened, she would get up and walk quietly through the apartment, examining everything: the second-hand furniture she had stripped and fixed, the wallpaper and the scenic mural she had painted depicting a green wooded area complete with a small brook. During those moments, quite alone, she experienced a sense of gratification and peacefulness which soothed both her body and spirit. Virginia would go back to bed, feeling that perhaps the wanderlust that had dominated her in the past was finally over. Besides, this time there are children. Virginia would smile and close her eyes. Papa and Mama are right, perhaps a small miracle has occurred.

"How long does it take to get two bottles of soda?" Mateo paced up and down the kitchen.

"We're hungry. When is mommy coming back?"

"She should've been back already. I don't know what the hell is keeping that woman. Wait . . . let's see what's she got on the stove? Hamburgers and . . . vegetable soup. Okay, I'll give you your food now."

"Hurry!" Sammy shouted, "I'm starving."

"Take it easy will you? Stop screaming!" Mateo fed his children and decided to wait a while longer before he ate. He sipped his beer watching Lillie and Sammy eat supper.

"I'm finished."

"Me too."

"What the hell is going on here?" He looked at the wall clock. "She's been gone for an hour and a half."

"Daddy . . . I'm finished."

"All right then, get ready for bed."

"I wanna watch television, Daddy, tonight there's this . . ."

"All right . . . all right, wash up first, go on . . . you too, Lillie."

"Where's Mommy?" Lillie asked.

"She went out for a little while, she'll be right back . . . go on, wash up, will you?"

Relunctantly, Mateo cleared the table and loaded the sink with dirty dishes and pots. "I don't understand what's going on here." The last quarrel they had was two days ago. Since then, they had hardly spoken a word to each other. Some ugly things had been said, and he had meant to make it up to Virginia. Maybe he should've told her he was sorry . . . but that was not his way.

"I'll call her mother, maybe she's there; that's it," he said out loud.

Mateo dialed and waited. "Hi, Mateo. Look, Mom, is Virginia there? No? She didn't come by at all? No, it's all right. No, don't worry. She just went out for a little bit and hasn't come back. What? Well, we had a fight and maybe that's it. I know . . . I know we shouldn't. Look, I don't have time now, I've gotta get the kids to bed. We'll work it out . . . sure, of course, we will, Mom, Virginia and I have been through this before. Thanks . . . yes. I'll let you know as soon as she returns. I'll tell her to call you. Bye . . . okay, thanks. Bye!"

"Daddy! Come here . . . Daddy . . ."

"Just a minute . . ."

Mateo helped the children wash up and put on their pajamas.

"Now, you can watch TV for another half hour, then to bed. You got school tomorrow, Sammy."

"Where's Mommy?"

"She's out. She'll be back soon, I told you. Go on, watch TV . . . don't bother me now."

Mateo checked the time once more. She was out almost three hours. "Maybe something happened to her . . . I better check it out."

"Look, kids. I'm going out for a few minutes to the store."

"Are you going to find Mommy?"

"Yeah. Now stay here watching television. Don't go into the kitchen or nothing like that. Okay?"

Outside it was cold and dark, the streets were desolate. He went into the local grocery and asked for Virginia. According to the owners, she had not been in all evening. Mateo checked the neighborhood supermarket; she was not there either. He decided to get back home; perhaps she was trying to call him.

"Any phone call, kids?"

"No, Daddy."

"Get to bed."

"Aww . . . come on, I want to see the end of this program . . . just a little . . ."

"Never mind . . ." Mateo turned off the set, "get to bed."

He helped them into their beds.

"Mommy always reads to us," Sammy said.

"Quit it will you, Sammy? You're getting to be a real pest. I'm not Mommy. I got things to do. She'll read to you when she gets back."

"What if she gets back and we're already sleeping?"

"Then . . . she'll read to you tomorrow. Good night."

"Aww . . . come on, Daddy . . . please."

"You wanna strap?" Mateo gestured, as if he were removing his belt. "No? All right then, go to sleep. And Lillie, stop that whining . . . or else!"

"Good night."

Mateo went to the telephone and waited. Maybe she's at Rickey's. I'll call there, but not right now . . . I'll wait another half-hour. Finally, he walked into their bedroom and turned on the light; something was wrong. Virginia's comb and brush set, her perfume, all her things were not on the bureau. Quickly he opened the closet; except for a sweater and a cotton dress, all her clothes were gone. He went through the drawers; she had taken all her personal belongings. Frantically he searched for a note, some kind of message from her, but there was nothing.

"Why?" he whispered, "why, Virginia?"

Mateo sat on the bed without moving. Things had been going badly between them, that's true, but he had been sure they could work it out; they always had. They had been together now for eight months . . . what happened? No note, no nothing. He found it hard to breathe; the pressure in his chest reached his throat and he let out a cry. Mateo covered his mouth with both hands, trying to restrain his sobs. After a few moments, he calmed down and felt a surge of tremendous anger overtake him.

"What about the kids, eh?" he cried out. "Damn it . . . Virginia, what about the kids?"

Virginia turned the key and opened the locker at the Port Authority Bus Terminal. She removed her suitcases. She checked her wristwatch. Almost time to board the bus . . . she rushed to gate 24, showed her ticket and found her seat on the bus.

"This the bus going to Los Angeles? Express bus?" she heard a man ask the driver.

"This is the one, mister."

She shut her eyes, feeling the motor start and the bus begin to move. Virginia opened her eyes, pressed the button on the arm of her chair until she was in a reclining position. She was still recovering from a nasty cold. She sneezed several times, wiped her eyes and blew her nose. Winter had brought flus, stomach viruses and colds, keeping the children at home for weeks on end. They had all felt like prisoners. Mateo had started staying out after work. "Just a few beers with the boys . . . gotta unwind, baby . . . I've had a rough day." And then he was hardly ever home evenings. Virginia watched the city as it swiftly disappeared.

"None of that matters to me anymore," she murmured. As they whizzed by Newark Airport, the bus sped past the large, ugly factories all lit up and spitting smoke.

Right now she should be putting the kids to bed; a cold shiver ran through her. Lillie would be asking for her. Lillie could not go to sleep unless Virginia sang to her. Virginia opened her handbag and popped two decongestant tablets and two sleeping pills into her mouth. Perhaps she would take another sleeping pill. They were an over-the-counter brand that she had purchased at the Port Authority drugstore. Yeah . . . one more wouldn't hurt. She wanted to shut her eyes and go to sleep. The straight steady movement of the bus and the darkness outside were almost hypnotic.

This week she had a parents meeting at shool about Sammy's behavior. He was an habitual liar. That boy! How many times had he told her he was in school and instead he was out playing hookey, and no matter how she tried to make him behave — talking, punishments, even bribes — nothing worked. Now she had to deal with that again! Then, tomorrow? Oh yes, tomorrow Lillie starts religious instructions for her first communion. She had to make sure Lillie got there on time and had to pick her up

before Sammy got home. The slipcovers were still at the dry
cleaners . . . Mateo had forgotten to pick them up again. Damn
him! Oh, and her parents were having them over for dinner this
Friday. She knew they would bring up the subject of marriage,
no matter how many times she told them not to. This time she
wasn't putting up with that crap . . . she was tired . . . of that
whole scene . . . her eyes became very heavy. Virginia yawned,
feeling drowsy.

This afternoon she had called Cornelia, confirming her exact
time of arrival in Los Angeles. They hadn't seen each other for
more than five years. Cornelia had a steady lover now, but still,
she had offered her a place to stay; just until Virginia could get
started again. Virginia smiled. Cornelia had been her first love.
From that very first time in class, Virginia had been drawn to
Cornelia. She would help Cornelia, staying after school, running errands. Virginia wanted to be near the gentle, attractive
woman. When Cornelia had given her a present, Virginia had
been overwhelmed. "Here's a present for you, Virginia. You
have been a tremendous help to me and a good friend. It's
Vivaldi's *The Four Seasons*: spring, summer, autumn and winter. Each musical piece represents one of these seasons. You are
in the springtime of your life. I'm in the beginning of my
autumn." She had played the record over and over. They had
become even better friends, seeing each other often. Virginia
visited Cornelia in her small, neat apartment, filled with all
kinds of books and pictures on the walls. It had been so beautiful
and comfortable between them, the discovering and sharing.
Virginia had not known many boys. Her parents had forbidden
her to socialize or go out with boys. "Thinking of sex before
marriage is a sin" was what her mother had told her. "You must
remain pure, until you meet someone who is serious and honor-
able. Then, when you marry this person, Virginia, and only
then, will it be right . . . with your husband. This is the way it
was with me and your father. You must do the same." She had felt
awkward and frightened with boys. Her two older brothers had

left home when she was still quite young, and she hardly knew them.

Virginia had fallen in love with Cornelia, totally and passionately. They could not bear to be separated and so they ran off together. Cornelia, fearful she would be traced, had given up her teaching career and started all over again as a proof-reader in a publishing house. Virginia had found work as a sales clerk in a book shop. They had lived together for five years, until there came a time when Virginia had wanted to break away from Cornelia and to have other lovers. She had found Sandy and a few others and then Tim. Tim was her first man, and for the short time they were together (less than six months), she had loved him very much. He had dark eyes like Lillie and he was thin and delicate too. But she hadn't wanted to marry and have children; so they had parted. After Tim, there had been a number of love affairs, some so brief that she could not even recall her lovers' names. It was just about two years later that Virginia had decided to come back east to see her parents. The idea of having a family, establishing firm roots and belonging somewhere appealed to her. Yes, she thought, she was not getting any younger. She had to stop running and searching . . . for what? She had to be able to call some place home.

Virginia's eyelids closed and the even movement of the bus made her sleepier. She remembered Tim again; he was so sweet, much like Lillie . . . dear little girl. Now, she was heading back at this time in her life . . . back to Cornelia.

"Spring, summer, autumn and winter," she murmured, realizing that she was approaching the end of her summer and soon would be entering her autumn — and then, what would she find there?

A Thanksgiving Celebration
(Amy)

A Thanksgiving Celebration
(Amy)

Amy sat on her bed thinking. Gary napped soundly in his crib, which was placed right next to her bed. The sucking sound he made as he chewed on his thumb interrupted her thoughts from time to time. Amy glanced at Gary and smiled. He was her constant companion now; he shared her bedroom and was with her during those frightening moments when, late into the night and early morning, she wondered if she could face another day just like the one she had safely survived. Amy looked at the small alarm clock on the bedside table. In another hour or so it would be time to wake Gary and give him his milk, then she had just enough time to shop and pick up the others, after school.

She heard the plopping sound of water dropping into a full pail. Amy hurried into the bathroom, emptied the pail into the toilet, then replaced it so that the floor remained dry. Last week she had forgotten, and the water had overflowed out of the pail and onto the floor, leaking down into Mrs. Wynn's bathroom. Now, Mrs. Wynn was threatening to take her to small claims court, if the landlord refused to fix the damage done to her bathroom ceiling and wallpaper. All right, Amy shrugged, she would try calling the landlord once more. She was tired of the countless phone calls to plead with them to come and fix the leak in the roof.

"Yes, Mrs. Guzman, we got your message and we'll send somebody over. Yes, just as soon as we can . . . we got other tenants with bigger problems, you know. We are doing our best, we'll get somebody over; you gotta be patient . . ."

Time and again they had promised, but no one had ever showed up. And it was now more than four months that she had been forced to live like this. Damn, Amy walked into her kitchen, they never refuse the rent for that, there's somebody ready any time! Right now, this was the best she could do. The building was still under rent control and she had enough room. Where else could she go? No one in a better neighborhood would rent to her, not the way things were.

She stood by the window, leaning her side against the molding, and looked out. It was a crisp sunny autumn day, mild for the end of November. She remembered it was the eve of Thanksgiving and felt a tightness in her chest. Amy took a deep breath, deciding not to worry about that right now.

Rows and rows of endless streets scattered with abandoned buildings and small houses stretched out for miles. Some of the blocks were almost entirely leveled, except for clumps of partial structures charred and blackened by fire. From a distance they looked like organic masses pushing their way out of the earth. Garbage, debris, shattered glass, bricks and broken, discarded furniture covered the ground. Rusting carcasses of cars that had been stripped down to the shell shone and glistened a bright orange under the afternoon sun.

There were no people to be seen nor traffic, save for a group of children jumping on an old filthy mattress that had been ripped open. They were busy pulling the stuffing out of the mattress and tossing it about playfully. Nearby, several stray dogs searched the garbage for food. One of the boys picked up a brick, then threw it at the dogs, barely missing them. Reluctantly, the dogs moved on.

Amy sighed and swallowed, it was all getting closer and closer. It seemed as if only last month, when she had looked out of this very window, all of that was much further away; in fact, she recalled feeling somewhat removed and safe. Now the decay was creeping up to this area. The fire engine sirens screeching and screaming in the night reminded her that the devastation was constant, never stopping even for a night's rest. Amy was fearful of living on the top floor. Going down four flights to safety with the kids in case of a fire was another source of worry for her. She remembered how she had argued with Charlie when they had first moved in.

"All them steps to climb with Michele and Carlito, plus carrying the carriage for Carlito, is too much."

"Come on baby," Charlie had insisted "it's only temporary. The rent's cheaper and we can save something towards buying our own place. Come on . . ."

That was seven years ago. There were two more children now, Lisabeth and Gary; and she was still here, without Charlie.

"Soon it'll come right to this street and to my doorstep. God Almighty!" Amy whispered. It was like a plague: a disease for which there seemed to be no cure, no prevention. Gangs of youngsters occupied empty store fronts and basements; derelicts, drunk or wasted on drugs, positioned themselves on street corners and in empty doorways. Every day she saw more abandoned and burned-out sections.

As Amy continued to look out, a feeling that she had been in this same situation before, a long time ago, startled her. The feeling of deja vu so real to her, reminded Amy quite vividly of the dream she had had last night. In that dream, she had been standing in the center of a circle of little girls. She herself was very young and they were all singing a rhyme. In a soft whisper, Amy sang the rhyme: "London Bridge is falling down, falling down, falling down, London Bridge is falling down, my fair lady . . . ." She stopped and saw herself once again in her dream, picking up her arms and chanting, "wave your arms and fly away, fly away, fly away . . ."

She stood in the middle of the circle waving her arms, first gently, then more forcefully, until she was flapping them. The other girls stared silently at her. Slowly, Amy had felt herself elevated above the circle, higher and higher until she could barely make out the human figures below. Waving her arms like the wings of a bird, she began to fly. A pleasant breeze pushed her gently, and she glided along, passing through soft white clouds into an intense silence. Then she saw it. Beneath her, huge areas were filled with crumbling buildings and large caverns; miles of destruction spread out in every direction. Amy had felt herself suspended in this silence for a moment and then she began to fall. She flapped her arms and legs furiously, trying to clutch at the air, hoping for a breeze, something to get her going again, but there was nothing. Quickly she fell, faster and faster, as the ground below her swirled and turned, coming closer and closer, revealing destroyed, burned buildings, rubble and a huge dark cavern. In a state of hysteria, Amy had fought against the loss of control and helplessness, as her body descended into the large black hole and had woken up with a start just before she hit bottom.

Amy stepped away from the window for a moment, almost out of breath as she recollected the fear she had felt in her dream. She walked over to the sink and poured herself a glass of water.

"That's it, Europe and the war," she said aloud. "In the movies, just like my dream."

Amy clearly remembered how she had sat as a very little girl in a local movie theatre with her mother and watched horrified at the scenes on the screen. Newsreels showed entire cities almost totally devastated. Exactly as it had been in her dream, she recalled seeing all the destruction caused by warfare. Names like "Munich, Nuremburg, Berlin" and "the German people" identified the areas. Most of the streets were empty, except for the occasional small groups of people who rummaged about, searching among the ruins and huge piles of debris, sharing the spoils with packs of rats who scavenged at a safe distance. Some people pulled wagons and baby carriages loaded with bundles and household goods. Others carried what they owned on their backs.

Amy remembered turning to her mother, asking, "What was

going on? Mami, who did this? Why did they do it? Who are those people living there?"

"The enemy, that's who," her mother had whispered emphatically. "Bad people who started the war against our country and did terrible things to other people and to us. That's where your papa was for so long, fighting in the army. Don't you remember, Amy?"

"What kinds of things, Mami? Who were the other people they did bad things to?"

"Don't worry about them things. These people got what they deserved. Besides, they are getting help from us, now that we won the war. There's a plan to help them, even though they don't deserve no help from us."

Amy had persisted, "Are there any little kids there? Do they go to school? Do they live in them holes?"

"Shh . . . let me hear the rest of the news . . ." her mother had responded, annoyed. Amy had sat during the remainder of the double feature, wondering where those people lived and all about the kids there. And she continued to wonder and worry for several days, until one day she forgot all about it.

Amy sipped from the glass she held, then emptied most of the water back into the sink. She sat and looked around at her small kitchen. The ceiling was peeling and flakes of paint had fallen on the kitchen table. The entire apartment was in urgent need of a thorough plastering and paint job. She blinked and shook her head, and now? Who are we now? What have I done? Who is the enemy? Is there a war? Are we at war? Amy suppressed a loud chuckle.

"Nobody answered my questions then, and nobody's gonna answer them now," she spoke out load.

Amy still wondered and groped for answers about Charlie. No one could tell her what had really happened . . . how he had felt and what he was thinking before he died. Almost two years had gone by, but she was still filled with an overwhelming sense of loneliness. That day was just like so many other days; they were together, planning about the kids, living from one crisis to the next, fighting, barely finding the time to make love without being exhausted; then late that night, it was all over. Charlie's late again, Amy had thought, and didn't even call me. She was angry when she heard the doorbell. He forgot the key again. Dammit, Charlie! You would forget your head if it weren't attached to you!

They had stood there before her; both had shown her their badges, but only one had spoken.

"Come in . . . sit down, won't you."

"You better sit down, miss." The stranger told her very calmly and soberly that Charlie was dead.

"On the Bruckner Boulevard Expressway . . . head on collision . . . dead on arrival . . . didn't suffer too long . . . nobody was with him, but we found his wallet."

Amy had protested and argued — No way! They were lying to her. But after a while she knew they brought the truth to her, and Charlie wasn't coming back.

Tomorrow would be the second Thanksgiving without him and one she could not celebrate. Celebrate with what? Amy stood and walked over and opened the refrigerator door. She had enough bread, a large pitcher of powdered milk which she had flavored with Hershey's cocoa and powdered sugar. There was plenty of peanut butter and some graham crackers she had kept fresh by sealing them in a plastic bag. For tonight she had enough chopped meat and macaroni. But tomorrow? What could she buy for tomorrow?

Amy shut the refrigerator door and reached over to the money tin set way back on one of the shelves. Carefully she took out the money and counted every cent. There was no way she could buy a turkey, even a small one. She still had to manage until the first; she needed every penny just to make it to the next check. Things were bad, worse than they had ever been. In the past, when things were rough, she had turned to Charlie and sharing had made it all easier. Now there was no one. She resealed the money tin and put it away.

Amy had thought of calling the lawyers once more. What good would that do? What can they do for me? Right now . . . today!

"These cases take time before we get to trial. We don't want to take the first settlement they offer. That wouldn't do you or the children any good. You have a good case, the other driver was at fault. He didn't have his license or the registration, and we have proof he was drinking. His father is a prominent judge who doesn't want that kind of publicity. I know . . . yes, things are rough, but just hold on a little longer. We don't want to accept a poor settlement and risk your future and the future of your children, do we?" Mr. Silverman of Silverman, Knapp and Ullman was handling the case personally. "By early Spring we should be making a date for trial . . . just hang in there a bit longer . . ." And so it went every time she called: the promise that in just a few more months she could hope for relief, some money, enough to live like people.

Survivor benefits had not been sufficient, and since they had not kept up premium payments on Charlie's G.I. insurance policy, she had no other income. Amy was given a little more assistance from the Aid to Dependent Children agency. Somehow she had managed so far.

The two food stores that extended her credit were still waiting for Amy to settle overdue accounts. In an emergency she could count on a few friends; they would lend her something, but not for this, not for Thanksgiving dinner.

She didn't want to go to Papo and Mary's again. She knew her brother meant well, and that she always had an open invitation. They're good people, but we are five more mouths to feed, plus they've been taking care of Papa all these years, ever since Mami died. Enough is enough. Amy shut her eyes. I want my own dinner this year, just for my family, for me and the kids.

If I had the money, I'd make a dinner tomorrow and invite Papa and Lou Ann from downstairs and her kids. She's been such a good friend to us. I'd get a gallon of cider and a bottle of wine . . . a large cake at the bakery by Alexander's, some dried fruits and nuts . . . even a holiday centerpiece for the table. Yes, it would be my dinner for us and my friends. I might even invite Jimmy. She hadn't seen Jimmy for a long time. Must be over six months . . . almost a year? He worked with Charlie at the plant. After Charlie's death, Jimmy had come by often, but Amy was not ready to see another man, not just then, so she discouraged him. From time to time, she thought of Jimmy and hoped he would visit her again.

Amy opened her eyes and a sinking feeling flowed through her, as she looked down at the chips of paint spread out on the kitchen table. Slowly, Amy brushed them with her hand, making a neat pile.

These past few months, she had seriously thought of going out to work. Before she had Michele, she had worked as a clerk-typist for a large insurance company, but that was almost ten years ago. She would have to brush up on her typing and math. Besides, she didn't know if she could earn enough to pay for a sitter. She couldn't leave the kids alone; Gary wasn't even three and Michele had just turned nine. Amy had applied for part-time work as a teacher's aide, but when she learned that her check from Aid to Dependent Children could be discontinued, she withdrew her application. Better to go on like this until the case comes to trial.

Amy choked back the tears. I can't let myself get like this. I just can't! Lately, she had begun to find comfort at the thought of never waking up again. What about my kids, then? I must do something. I have to. Tomorrow is going to be for us, just us, our day.

Her thoughts went back to her own childhood and the holiday dinners with her family. They had been poor, but there was always food. We used to have such good times. Amy remembered the many stories her grandmother used to tell them. She spoke about her own childhood on a farm in a rural area of

Puerto Rico. Her grandmother's stories were about the animals, whom she claimed to know personally and very well. Amy laughed, recalling that most of the stories her grandmother related were too impossible to be true, such as a talking goat who saved the town from a flood, and the handsome mouse and beautiful lady beetle who fell in love, got married and had the biggest and fanciest wedding her grandmother had ever attended. Her grandmother was very old and had died before Amy was ten. Amy had loved her best, more than her own parents, and she still remembered the old woman quite clearly.

"Abuelita, did them things really happen? How come them animals talked? Animals don't talk. Everybody knows that."

"Oh, but they do talk! And yes, everything I tell you is absolutely the truth. I believe it and you must believe it too." The old woman had been completely convincing. And for many years Amy had secretly believed that when her grandmother was a little girl, somewhere in a special place, animals talked, got married and were heroes.

"Abuelita," Amy whispered, "I wish you were here and could help me now." And then she thought of it. Something special for tomorrow. Quickly, Amy took out the money tin, counting out just the right amount of money she needed. She hesitated for a moment. What if it won't work and I can't convince them? Amy took a deep breath. Never mind, I have to try, I must. She counted out a few more dollars. I'll work it all out somehow. Than she warmed up Gary's milk and got ready to leave.

Amy heard the voices of her children with delight. Shouts and squeals of laughter bounced into the kitchen as they played in the living room. Today they were all happy, anticipating their mother's promise of a celebration. Recently, her frequent moods of depression and short temper had frightened them. Privately, the children had blamed themselves for their mother's unhappiness, fighting with each other in helpless confusion. The children welcomed their mother's energy and good mood with relief.

Lately Amy had begun to realize that Michele and Carlito

were constantly fighting. Carlito was always angry and would
pick on Lisabeth. Poor Lisabeth, she's always so sad. I never
have time for her and she's not really much older than Gary. This
way of life has been affecting us all . . . but not today. Amy
worked quickly. The apartment was filled with an air of festivity.
She had set the kitchen table with a paper tablecloth, napkins
and paper cups to match. These were decorated with turkeys,
pilgrims, Indian corn and all the symbols of the Thanksgiving
holiday. Amy had also bought a roll of orange paper streamers
and decorated the kitchen chairs. Each setting had a name-card
printed with bright magic markers. She had even managed to
purchase a small holiday cake for dessert.

As she worked, Amy fought moments of anxiety and fear that
threatened to weaken her sense of self-confidence. What if they
laugh at me? Dear God in heaven, will my children think I'm a
fool? But she had already spent the money, cooked and arranged
everything; she had to go ahead. If I make it through this day,
Amy nodded, I'll be all right.

She set the food platter in the center of the table and stepped
back. A mound of bright yellow rice, flavored with a few spices
and bits of fatback, was surrounded by a dozen hardboiled eggs
that had been colored a bright orange. Smiling, Amy felt it was
all truly beautiful; she was ready for the party.

"All right," Amy walked into the living room. "We're
ready!" The children quickly followed her into the kitchen.

"Oooh, Mommy," Lisabeth shouted, "everything looks so
pretty."

"Each place has got a card with your own name, so find the
right seat." Amy took Gary and sat him down on his special
chair next to her.

"Mommy," Michele spoke, "is this the whole surprise?"

"Yes," Amy answered, "just a minute, we also have some
cider." Amy brought a small bottle of cider to the table.

"Easter eggs for Thanksgiving?" Carlito asked.

"Is that what you think they are, Carlito?" Amy asked.

"Because they are not Easter eggs."

The children silently turned to one another, exchanging bewildered looks.

"What are they?" Lisabeth asked.

"Well," Amy said, "these are . . . turkey eggs, that's what. What's better than a turkey on Thanksgiving day? Her eggs, right?" Amy continued as all of them watched her. "You see, it's not easy to get these eggs. They're what you call a delicacy. But I found a special store that sells them, and they agreed to sell me a whole dozen for today."

"What store is that, Mommy?" Michele asked. "Is it around here?"

"No. They don't have stores like that here. It's special, way downtown."

"Did the turkey lay them eggs like that? That color?" Carlito asked.

"I want an egg," Gary said pointing to the platter.

"No, no . . . I just colored them that way for today, so everything goes together nicely, you know . . ." Amy began to serve the food. "All right, you can start eating."

"Well then, what's so special about these eggs? What's the difference between a turkey egg and an egg from a chicken?" Carlito asked.

"Ah, the taste, Carlito, just wait until you have some." Amy quickly finished serving everyone. "You see, these eggs are hard to find because they taste so fantastic." She chewed a mouthful of egg. "Ummm . . . fantastic, isn't it?" She nodded at them.

"Wonderful, Mommy," said Lisabeth. "It tastes real different."

"Oh yeah," Cariito said, "you can taste it right away. Really good."

Everyone was busy eating and commenting on how special the eggs tasted. As Amy watched her children, a sense of joy filled her, and she knew it had been a very long time since they had been together like this, close and loving.

"Mommy, did you ever eat these kinds of eggs before?" asked Michele.

"Yes, when I was little," she answered. "My grandmother got them for me. You know, I talked about my abuelita before. When I first ate them, I couldn't get over how good they tasted, just like you." Amy spoke with assurance, as they listened to every word she said. "Abuelita lived on a farm when she was very little. That's how come she knew all about turkey eggs. She used to tell me the most wonderful stories about her life there."

"Tell us!"

"Yeah, please Mommy, please tell us."

"All right, I'll tell you one about a hero who saved her whole village from a big flood. He was . . . a billy goat."

"Mommy," Michele interrupted, "a billy goat?"

"That's right, and you have to believe what I'm going to tell you. All of you have to believe me. Because everything I'm going to say is absolutely the truth. Promise? All right, then, in the olden days, when my grandmother was very little, far away in a small town in Puerto Rico . . ."

Amy continued, remembering stories that she had long since forgotten. The children listened, intrigued by what their mother had to say. She felt a calmness within. Yes, Amy told herself, today's for us, for me and the kids.

Happy Birthday
(Lucia)

Happy Birthday
(Lucia)

Lucia lay in her hospital bed and waited anxiously. She tried to get the nurse's attention. She wanted someone to prop her bed up, so that she could have a better view of the entrance into the ward. Lucia saw one of the nurses at the far end of the ward and waited patiently. She knew better than to press the service button located near the side wall of her bed. That only irritated the nurses, and if one did come to do what Lucia asked, there might be hell to pay later. It all depended on the nurse and her mood at the time. Often, after Lucia complained or insisted that some small favor be done, she found her dinner would be ice cold that evening, or her dessert missing. Simple and small everyday requests, such as more water or the need for a bedpan, might be ignored. Once, when she was very weak and cried out for service, Lucia had to wait several days before she could get a change of bedclothes and a sponge bath. By now, Lucia had learned how to wait, and how to be patient and very polite.

The nurse was examining several bed charts and when she finished, she walked toward Lucia's part of the ward. Slowly, and with effort, Lucia pushed herself forward and with her free hand, waved to the nurse. The nurse saw her and nodded, then turned and went in the other direction. After several moments, the nurse approached Lucia.

"What do you want?"

"Please, raise the bed, nurse; on top here."

Without looking at Lucia, the nurse cranked up the bed, raising the upper part of Lucia's body, so that she was now in a comfortable elevated position.

"Enough?"

"Yes. Thank you very much Miss nurse Heller."

Lucia sighed, feeling better; now she had a good view of the entrance. There were thirty-six beds in this large ward. Eighteen beds were placed against opposite walls, creating a center aisle fourteen feet wide and over one hundred feet long. All the patients in this ward were chronically ill. Most of them had terminal cancer, except for a few like Lucia; they had advanced cases of tuberculosis.

"Hemoptysis and cavities . . ." the doctor had told her. She had not taken proper care of herself and now would have to face being "a terminal case with severe progression and hemorrhaging." Lucia had listened and thanked him for all his help and for all the staff was doing for her. She had no family and so the doctor had been frank and honest.

Lucia's bed was placed closer to the end wall near the huge window, which overlooked the grounds and shrubbery of Welfare Island, the murky waters of the East River, and part of the concrete gray silhouette of Manhattan's upper East Side. Lucia turned from the window and looked around at the other women. Most of them were quiet; napping, reading or just resting. The small clock on top of her side table showed the time to be 12:30. Today was Sunday and lunch had been served early so that visiting hours could be extended for an additional hour. Of course, Lucia reminded herself, everyone's resting after lunch. Visiting hours were usually from two to three in the afternoon, and from seven to eight in the evening. Today, the hours were from one to three in the afternoon and from seven to nine this evening. Except for the new patient being admitted and accompanied by a friend or relation, or the vigil of relatives over a dying patient, there was no contact with the outside world during the week. But

Sundays, the ward was lively with visitors and most of the women were in much better spirits . . .

Lucia glanced at the woman to the right of her. She lay back with her eyes shut and her mouth partially open, emitting a soft and even snore. Today was a happy day for her; her husband and daughter were sure to come. They never missed a Sunday; just like clockwork. Lucia turned to her other neighbor on the left. She had her back to Lucia. Her hair had become untied and was sticking out of her head like puffs of black cotton. Her dark brown arm was thrown casually over her hip contrasting against the whiteness of the sheets. Lucia smiled. Roxanne was always in a good mood. But she lived for Sundays, when her family brought her lots of food. "Girl, when the powers that be give me a reprieve, I'm gonna eat good every day of my life!" Roxanne believed she would get well. She was a devout Evangelist, and on Sundays, after she had eaten, her family would join her in prayer for most of the visits. "Believe in Him, Lucia. You got to have faith . . . faith in Him, Lucia. You got to have faith . . . faith in Him. For He shall save you if you trust and believe." Everyday Roxanne preached and proselytized to the other patients. Few listened, except for Lucia, and so they had become friends.

Lucia looked up at the large unit that held the clear intravenous liquid and watched the fluid rhythmically bubbling as it went through the thin plastic tube and into the needle taped securely in her left forearm. With her free hand, she reached over to the bedside cabinet and opened a small drawer. She found her comb, brush, make-up kit, hand mirror and small bottle of Tabu perfume. She still had time to freshen up her make-up and make sure she looked her best for him. Lucia was positive he would be here today. Today was special.

She rolled her tray stand toward her, set up her hand mirror. Carefully she combed and brushed her hair, applied a light film of soft powder over her rouged cheeks before putting on some more lipstick. Lucia looked at her image and bit her lip with disappointment. The make-up didn't hide the shallow tone of her dark skin which appeared ashen in spots. The dark circles under her light hazel eyes made them look so transparent and sunken, that it seemed to her, if she touched the back of her head, she would feel her eye sockets. Lucia closed her eyes. God, she was so very thin. Had she lost so much weight? She placed her hand on her chest, pressing the small gold medal of the Immaculate Conception that hung on a thin chain around her neck. Lucia felt the hardness of her collar-bone as it protruded through her hospital bedgown; then she felt her breasts. They were like two pieces of tissue paper, limp and lifeless. She removed the top of her perfume bottle and dabbed the scent sparingly behind her ears and on her throat. What a sight he's gonna see today . . . if he comes. Lucia shook her head. I'm not even gonna think like that. He'll be here. "By the time your birthday comes around, I'll be out to see you, baby. You get yourself well again, okay? You got to get looking better, mami, and we'll celebrate your next birthday together." Eddie had promised and today was her birthday. She had written countless long, passionate letters to Eddie. Most had been returned and there had been no response to the few he might have received.

Lucia wished she could have stayed in the city. It was easier for people to visit her when she was in Manhattan. At the beginning, the girls had come, from time to time, and Eddie's mother had been to see her once. Since Lucia had been transferred to Walfare Island, no one had been out to see her.

Lucia felt very tired and thirsty. She put her personal things away and picked up the glass of water that was on the table. It was warm and tasted of chlorine. She searched for a nurse, hoping to get some fresh water. It was very quiet; no one was about. She put the glass back and decided to nap for a few minutes. She checked the clock; it was twenty minutes to one. Lucia leaned back against the pillow and looked over at the large window. It was divided into many small window panes; exactly thirty-six, one for each bed Lucia had decided, as she counted them over and over again. First vertically, then horizontrally, obliquely and from every angle she could discover. It was a freezing cold February day. Ice had formed on the panes, developing into delicate shapes that appeared like leaves, flowers and lace patterns. The ice sparkled like diamonds as the long beams of the bright winter sunlight passed through the windows and splashed into the ward, creating large shadowy areas on the gray-green walls. She smiled, how beautiful it all was. Lucia realized that if she concentrated on the sparkling panes and shadows, she could separate herself from the ward. Lucia felt a warmth and happiness that reminded her of the beautiful riverbed in her mountain village in Sierra de Luquillo where as a little girl she used to bathe and play with her brother.

That part of the river was tucked safely into the side of a steep mountain and partially shaded by ferns, shrubs and wild flowers. She used to sit for hours just watching the tiny darting fish and tadpoles, the bobbing twigs and dry leaves as the tropical sun bounced on the water making them sparkle like jewels. Lucia felt mesmerized by the movement of all these tiny things being transported through the sluices of shallow water that had been formed by the rocks and fallen branches. She loved that part of the river. It had all been magical, wonderful, and belonged to her, until the day she began to bleed in the water. At first she and her little brother thought it was leeches that had gotten into her skin, and then they thought she had been cut by something. But the blood seemed to be coming from inside her body and for no reason at all. Frightened, she and her little brother ran all the way home. Confused and bewildered, Lucia had listened to her mother who forbade her to bathe or swim at that end of the river. From that day on she was to go in at the side of the river with the other women. Lucia was now a woman. Her grandmother had put her arms gently around Lucia, rocking her and from time to time stroking her hair, as she whispered in a soft voice, "My little brand new virgin . . . Lucia, my sweet little precious virgin . . . just born, my little virgin." Lucia, perplexed, had not understood until later, much later, when she had given herself freely and openly to Manuel, just before the departure. Afterward, she had cried and Manuel vowed that he would always respect her and someday they would be legally husband and wife.

Lucia's eyes were almost completely shut as she concentrated on the dark shadows spread across the walls of the ward and remembered the departure. She was going into service as a domestic. And, early that day, her new employers arrived. They had been in such a great hurry, that they had remained in the car. The wife had explained that they were in the process of closing their home in San Juan because, in two weeks' time, they would be leaving for New York City. Lucia barely had time to say good-bye to her parents, grandmother and little brother. The man and his wife sat in the front seat of the black limousine, and she sat in the back. She had wanted to open the window and say some-thing, shout or wave, but had no idea how to do it, and she was afraid to touch anything in that splendid car. Lucia gripped the twine tied tightly around the cardboard box that occupied the seat next to hers. Her clothes and possessions had been neatly packed in the box by her mother. The last glimpse of her family, and Manuel, standing by the side of the road wearing his best clothes as he waved goodbye, was etched in her memory.

The car had sped quickly out of her village and her fright intensified as she saw the capital city for the first time. Cars, trucks, large buildings and people were as abundant as the flies that swarmed around the pigpen. Lucia remembered the cold shiver that had passed right through her when she realized that she was going even farther away in two weeks and that she might never again see the trees and foliage of the quiet mountain region which had been the only world she had ever known.

"Ssst . . . sst . . . Lucia." She opened her eyes and saw him. His large dark eyes were staring at her. "How are you? How are you feeling, Lucia?" Somehow he looked different and it didn't sound like Eddie. "Lucia, ¿como estas?" Doña Nora was smil-ing at her. Reaching over, she patted Lucia's hand. "Are you all right, child?"

"Yes . . ." Lucia blinked. "Doña Nora, I thought . . . I thought at first," she hesitated.

"Thought what?"

"It might be Eddie. Eddie was supposed to come today."

"Today? You heard from him, then? Did he say he was coming?"

"No. Bueno . . . not exactly."

"Then, what . . ."

"He promised me when I left, you know, when I got sick, that he would come . . . he would see me before today was over."

"Child, that was more than six months ago. Nobody has seen that son of mine and nobody knows where he is. When I saw you last time, in the hospital back in the city, I told you that he had left New York. He was in trouble again. You know how Eddie is . . . Lucia, by now you should know."

"But he's different with me, Doña Nora. You know it was . . ." Lucia's voice had a sharpness as she continued, "I never was like the rest!"

"I know . . ." Doña Nora answered in a soft voice. She stared at Lucia for a moment, as if she were really seeing her for the first time, today. "I know you were not like the rest. We all knew and know that, Lucia."

"All right then," Lucia nodded at Doña Nora. "I only did what I had to . . . until, until Eddie could get the money he needed to set up a business. There were a lot of sacrifices we had to go through. But we were gonna get married. That was our goal, Eddie's and mine. It still is . . . someday . . . I . . ."

"Of course," Doña Nora interrupted her, speaking quickly. "Look, look what I brought for you, Lucia." She lifted a large shopping bag and placed it on a chair. "See, all homemade, eh? I just finished it this morning. Chicken broth with a nice piece of white meat. Here, I have some viandas: platanos, malanga, yautia, batata, and a piece of . . ."

Lucia watched Doña Nora and smiled as she took out jars and

plastic bowls filled with things to eat. "That's so much food; you are still the same, Doña Nora, thank you. You shouldn't have gone to such trouble."

"Nonsense, it's not so much. Anyway, I have to cook for my family. Besides, all of this will help you get well again faster; you'll see."

"I don't know, Doña Nora, I don't think I'm getting well again."

"What a thing to say! Not getting well? Shame! Don't talk like that!" Doña Nora shook her head. "Of course you're gonna get well! Good as new again. You're young, child, and the young heal quickly."

"I'm not young no more . . ." Lucia looked at Doña Nora. "And I don't heal fast."

"What? What are you saying? You are . . . why how old can you be? Twenty-four or twenty-five at the most. Eh?"

"Twenty. Today I'm twenty years old, Doña Nora."

"Twenty?"

"Yes, today is my birthday, Doña Nora."

"Today. Well, there, you see? Had I known, I would have gotten you a present . . ." Doña Nora's voice faded and she found that she could not look at Lucia. Quickly, she turned her head and looked around at the other patients. "My, look at how busy it is today in here. Lots of people visiting."

"All I wanted for today, Doña Nora, was to see him once. That's all. Once before I die."

"Die? Stop that, you are not going to die; you'll get well. But, you must stop talking like that. Think of the future, of what's ahead of you. You have your whole life before you. Lucia, don't talk about . . . talk about living."

"You know, Vickie and Carmen used to come to see me when I was in City Hospital, and I told them just how I felt. They had left Eddie by then, but anyway, they understood. Maybe, because we were all so close. They knew I was different from them. They always told me so. With them it was just a business because if it wasn't Eddie, it would be somebody else. But with me, there was never nobody else but him." Lucia stopped speaking and lowered her voice, continuing almost in a whisper, "When I was with other men, well . . . I never got used to it, and I never liked it." Lucia turned her head away and shut her eyes. "I hope you believe me, Doña Nora."

"Why do you think I'm here today, Lucia? Because I know you are different from those other women. They are professionals. Whores in that kind of business! But, not you, I know it was because of Eddie you got into that life. I even remember when he first brought you to see us. You were so shy and respectful. I knew then you were different. He even said to me, 'Ma, she's different! This one's a good girl.' And, I was happy. I thought he was going to settle down and stop what he was doing. But . . . instead, Dios mio, I don't understand Eddie. He's my son, but he's not like the rest of my children, God! I don't know why he's that way. So ruthless and uncaring. I don't know what I did or maybe what I didn't do. Could be that he was the oldest and had too much responsibility for the rest of the kids. And, he never got along with his stepfather . . ." Doña Nora hesitated and waited a moment for Lucia to respond. Lucia remained perfectly still, her head turned away and her eyes closed. "Oh my God . . . Lucia, what did I do to have such a son that he can do this to you? Look, I'm trying to make it up to you in some way. Let me help you, Lucia, let me try to help you. Look at you, you're so young . . . don't do this. Bendito, Lucia, don't give up like this. Please." Doña Nora's voice began to quiver and she cried quietly. After a moment she wiped her eyes and drew a deep breath. "I don't know where he is. I never know where he is. Sometimes, the police come for him. Sometimes, there's some strange woman, a prostitute, or some man who's after him. I don't know how long I can love my son. There are times I hate him! I hate him so much I want to see him dead . . ." She held back the tears, and with effort, continued, "not just because of you, but because of all he's put me and the family

through. Did you know he hid drugs in our house? That he gave
his younger brothers a gun to hide? A loaded pistol! Dear Virgin
Mary, I can't cope with him no more. Right now, I never want to
see him again. I think his being alive is more of a torture to me
than if he were dead!" Doña Nora broke into sobs and covered
her face with her hands.

"Doña Nora . . ." Lucia reached over and gently touched the
older woman's arm. "Don't! You see, he didn't force me. Don't
think that. I knew what it was all about. He told me how it was. I
did what I did because I wanted to. I'm not sorry about loving
Eddie, you know, only about some of the things I did."

Doña Nora wiped her eyes and face and looked silently at
Lucia. After a moment, she spoke in a calm voice. "Ay,
Lucia . . . you can still love him? You didn't hear what I said
and you don't see, do you?"

"I see. But, with me, he's different. He was really changing
with me. Perhaps, if I hadn't gotten so sick, things would be
better with him. I understood Eddie and what he wanted."

"All right, Lucia, let me help you. Let me contact your family. I can write to them. They will want to know where you are
and what is happening to you."

"No . . ." Lucia hesitated, "I don't want them to know."

"But, child, why?"

"Please, Doña Nora. I don't want to talk about them. Look, I
appreciate your coming to see me and whatever you do for me,
but . . . I don't want to talk about my family."

"You are being foolish not to let your people know."

"It's better like this."

"How can you say that? They are your family after all, and
your parents should know where and how you are."

"No."

"I don't agree, Lucia."

"Doña Nora, it's better like this. Like you, with Eddie, I
don't want them to wish me dead!"

"Oh! That was cruel," Doña Nora gasped. "I'm surprised at

you!"

"Let's leave things as they are."

Both women looked at each other silently. Doña Nora was the first to turn away.

"I'm sorry, I forgot to ask about the kids. How are they, Doña Nora? And, Don Luis, is he better?"

"Yes, he's a little better with his asthma. It's hard when he's not working, because they dock his pay. You know, there's just so many sick days allowed. And, the kids are fine. Frankie is graduating and Gilberto is doing good too. Linda is getting all grown up. In fact, I have to keep a sharp eye out in her direction, she just got her period."

Lucia continued to ask questions about Doña Nora's family, and the two women spoke politely and quietly until the loud speaker interrupted.

"VISITING HOURS ARE OVER. VISITORS, PLEASE LEAVE THE HOSPITAL. VISITING HOURS ARE . . ."

"Do you need anything, Lucia?" Doña Nora opened her purse and took out three dollars. "Here . . ."

"No . . . thank you, you've done enough."

"It's okay. Take it. You were very kind to my kids. Giving them presents and all . . . go on."

"Thank you." Lucia took the money and put it in the drawer of her bedside table. "I could use some toothpaste and talc."

"Goodbye, then." Doña Nora picked up her empty shopping bag and carefully folded it. "If you need anything, let us know."

"I will. Thank you for coming and for the things you brought me."

"VISITING HOURS ARE OVER. VISITORS, PLEASE LEAVE . . ."

"Well, I better go, it's a trip back to Brooklyn from here . . ."

"Doña Nora?"

"Yes?"

"Don't hate him. Don't hate Eddie, please."

"It's all right, Lucia. I don't hate Eddie. I only hate what he's become. I just don't know if I still have a son . . . that's all. Bueno . . . never mind all that. You try to get well."

"Thank you."

"Goodbye, Lucia."

"Goodbye, Doña Nora."

"Oh . . . Lucia."

"Yes?"

"Happy Birthday."

Lucia nodded and smiled as she watched the older woman walk toward the large open doorway and disappear. She checked the time once more. It was twenty minutes past three. There's still tonight, and it's still my birthday. She looked at all the food Doña Nora had brought. Later she would try to eat some. Right now she was tired. Lucia closed her eyes. Lately, Eddie and Manuel got all mixed up in her mind. She could not really separate them; even their features blended together until they appeared as one person. It was too confusing and she was too exhausted to think about all that, instead she would go back and bathe in her riverbed. Lucia concentrated once more and saw the clear, transparent water and the swift movement of her hand as she tried to grab a tadpole. The cool water splashed her face, running down her neck and body. Lucia stepped into the river and felt the water envelop her. She turned and swam toward the deeper part. Slowly, and without any resistance, Lucia let the current take her downstream and she drifted with the river into a journey of quiet bliss.

Welfare Island — 1954

The Artist
(Inez)

The Artist
(Inez)
Part 1

When Inez Otero reached her eighteenth birthday, she had already been married for over six months. At first the reality that marriage would take her out of and far away from the Vasquez household seemed to her, not only to be a stroke of extraordinary good luck in her life, but a minor miracle. This was because, ever since Inez was eleven years old, she had prayed every night fervently to God that somehow and in some way she would be set free from the miserable life she had been forced into. For it was soon after her eleventh birthday when her mother died, that Inez had been taken in by her Aunt Ofelia, her late father's older sister. Inez' brother Frankie, seventeen at that time, had opted to join the air force — a better fate, he had decided, than to live under the same roof with his pernicious Aunt Ofelia. Frankie seldom wrote to his little sister; in time her letters to him went unanswered. The years passed and brother and sister lost touch with each other. By the time she was sixteen, Inez was feeling completely abandoned and very much alone in the world.

And . . . so it was no wonder that when Joe Batista — divorced, attractive, aged thirty-one, with a good steady job as a bus dispatcher for the City of New York, and a night student at St. John's University — proposed marriage, Inez did not even hesitate to catch her breath as she responded, "Oh yes, thank you," and heaved a sigh of relief.

Marrying, living in her own apartment far away from the Vasquez family, and being independent once and for all, Inez decided, was a sure path to a happy future. This way, she reasoned, she would be able to work and study art, a desire she had been nourishing ever since she was a child. Inez was one of those individuals who was blessed with a natural ability for drawing and painting. These were the skills that had set her apart from most other children. In school she always had her drawings displayed in the halls and library.

Whenever things took a turn for the worst, Inez would recall her late mother's words: "*Mi hijita*, my little daughter, you are special with these God-given talents. Someday you must study so that you can become an important artist . . . make an important contribution to the world and really be somebody." This always made her feel better. She would turn to her pencil, crayons and paper, and create something pleasing, even amusing, where previously all there had been was a sense of dispair. Her burden then became lighter and she was better able to cope. Always when she was humiliated or abused, she would take out her drawings and look at them, feeling a sense of self-worth. Knowing she was an artist and not like "ordinary people" enabled her to build a strong emotional barrier that protected her from being spiritually defeated or brought down into submission by her evil Aunt. Consequently, the desire to study art someday had become an obsession with Inez.

However, in the six months since her marriage, Inez had only experienced what it was to be Joe Batista's wife. That independence she expected, and studying art, were still beyond her reach. To make matters worse, Joe Batista turned out to be an insanely jealous man, and almost as stingy as Aunt Ofelia. Of course, she had only known Joe just a little over four months before she had married him. Still, during these six months, Inez had saved enough money to begin planning where she would study art, despite her husband's disapproval, and how she could once again change her life. Inez now wondered if the old saying, "from the frying pan into the fire," did after all apply to her decision to become Joe's wife. And yet, although life with her husband was not what she had expected, she was not sorry she had managed to escape from living under the same roof with Aunt Ofelia.

Aunt Ofelia was a tiny but plump woman who was shaped like a pear. She had beady eyes and thin delicate extremities. Her hands, fingers, feet and toes resembled claws. Inez had once observed the sandpiper bird at the beach as it bounced along the shore, taking tiny steps and greedily sticking it's beak in the sand searching for food. "Why that looks just like Aunt Ofelia!" she had whispered to herself. After returning home that very day, she had made a caricature of Aunt Ofelia as a sandpiper.

Having the nature of a true miser, Aunt Ofelia's avariciousness extended to everyone, including her own children. No one was ever given more food, shelter and clothing than was necessary. No one starved or went naked . . . but under the auspices of Aunt Ofelia, more than that was not possible. However, her greediness was especially vicious when it came to Inez. For example, Inez always got skimpier portions of food than did anyone else. When her own children requested second helpings, Aunt Ofelia reluctantly obliged them. Not so with Inez, who by now knew better than to even ask for more food.

Aunt Ofelia was also given to making long-winded speeches to anyone who would listen about her generosity for taking in, feeding and clothing her dead brother's orphaned daughter.

"You don't know how much she costs me," she would say. "Why, it takes so much money to meet all the needs of a growing girl who eats all the time and outgrows her clothes practically by the week. But, poor thing has no other relatives here. Her mother's people are all in Puerto Rico and they don't want her. I'm my dead brother's only sister . . . so what could I do? Her mother died a pauper and so the girl came to me penniless. Even her own brother Frankie left and doesn't care about her. I'm the only one she has, *pobrecita*, poor little thing. Still, when I have to pay for everything and what with inflation and the prices of things these days . . . it's a great sacrifice to provide for her. Nevertheless, I'm a good Christian and I believe in almighty

God . . . so I treat Inez as if she were my very own daughter, just like my Diedre and Papito."

Actually Aunt Ofelia was so stingy that she hated to part with even a penny, and so she never threw anything out. She saved empty bottles, plastic containers, string, paper and plastic bags, rubberbands, boxes, ribbons, used gifts and wrapping paper, corks . . . the list was endless. On those rare occasions when she went to buy new clothes, Aunt Ofelia did so only after having first searched in the Goodwill Industries, the Salvation Army and all the second-hand clothing shops she could find.

Uncle Generoso, Aunt Ofelia's husband, was a small thin man with a sallow complexion and he was bald as a cue ball. He worked as a merchant marine who preferred to sign up for long voyages that kept him away at sea for months at a time. When his wife complained about those long absences from home, he would outline all the benefits derived. "Why, look how much money I make this way. I get paid extra bonuses for holidays and for overtime duty. We don't have to spend money on my clothes . . . you don't have to feed me and look after me. It's the only way we can really save money." With this kind of economic philosophy, Aunt Ofelia needed very little convincing.

Whenever his family complained about life on land without the protection and moral support of a husband and father, Uncle Generoso would listen, smile, cock his bald head from side to side, and make his one and only comment, "I know . . . tch, tch. What can one do, then? It's really a shame," which he repeated to anyone and in defense of any new arguments that were presented to him.

All the presents he brought home were immediately confiscated by Aunt Ofelia. She alone would decide who and when, and if anyone got anything at all. In all the years that Inez had lived with them, she had been given only two of the presents that had been bought for her. One was a small bottle of toilet water from France, and the other was a purple and green silk scarf from Italy. During his short visits home, Uncle Generoso read the newspapers, watched T.V., and was in bed promptly by seven-thirty in the evenings (even on weekends). He somehow also maneuvered his way out of having conversations with anybody. Knowing from past disappointments that it was useless to try, Inez had given up trying to ask her Uncle to intercede on her behalf and persuade Aunt Ofelia to act more humanely towards her. In fact, as the years went by, Uncle Generoso was increasingly ignored by everyone.

Cousin Diedre, who was six months younger than Inez, lived her life in a state of perpetual insecurity. She had acquired a disagreeable habit of whining when she spoke and was given to indulging in long fits of crying. Since the two girls shared a bedroom, Diedre's crying would sometimes keep Inez up until all hours of the night. Nonetheless, Cousin Diedre did have two redeeming qualities and these were that she had not inherited her mother's greediness and that she disliked her own family almost as much as Inez did. However, because of her weak character, Diedre depended on Inez for moral support. She would have temper tantrums insisting that Inez give her undivided attention to the complaints and grievances she had against her mother, father and brother. When Inez still refused to listen, Diedre would offer her a bribe: an item of clothing, sweets, money, almost anything to get her attention. Sometimes Inez gave in to temptation, accepting Diedre's bribes, but most of the time she refused. Instead, Inez lost herself in her artwork and ignored her cousin. Although Inez had a certain fondness for Diedre, she also felt contempt and a lack of respect for her. Very often Inez longed for the day when she didn't have to share a room with "tearie dearie," which was her secret nickname for Diedre. Inez had made several caricatures of Diedre as a twisted weeping willow tree tearing out her own limbs, as a frightened mouse tried to decide which hole to hide in. Another one had been of Diedre hysterically drowning in her own pool of tears and mucous.

But if there was anyone in that household that Inez truly despised complete with the desire to murder him, it was cousin

Papo, four years her junior and the apple of his mother's eye. Nothing was too good for the viciously spoiled "Papito," as his mother called him. If there was a trace of generosity in Aunt Ofelia's heart, it was all spent on her son, who was mean-spirited and self-centered. For instance, from an early age, Papo had developed an obnoxious habit of pointing to what it was he wanted, never uttering a word. If his wish were not quickly attended to, which was not easy to do since one could not always guess what he wanted, cousin Papo would begin screaming by calling out his mother's Christian name, "Ofelia — Ofelia — Ofelia — Ofelia — !!!" He wouldn't stop until his mother arrived in an agitated state. This meant that whoever hadn't done Papo's bidding might be punished in several ways: being deprived of lunch or supper, perhaps made to clean the toilet, or even being grounded. When Inez first came to live with them, she had made the mistake of smacking Papo around a few times. This resulted in Inez being locked in a dark closet for hours, and more than once she had been made to sit at the dinner table in silence with her hands folded until everyone had finished eating. She would then be excused in order to clean up and wash the dishes. Very quickly Inez learned that it didn't pay to tangle with cousin Papo and that, no matter how terribly he behaved, it was best to ignore him.

At night alone in her bed, Inez would fantasize choking Papo with her bare hands or beating him to death with a long black whip. She cherished and kept alive in her mind the memories of her mother. She would wish for some miracle that would make her mother appear and take her out of there. Memories of her father were vague, since he had died when she was only five years old. Sometimes Inez imagined that he wasn't dead at all and that he might even turn up at the front door. He would be strong and handsome and bring lots of gifts for her. Then he would scold Aunt Ofelia, Uncle Generoso, cousin Diedre and cousin Papo, making them all ashamed of the way they mistreated her. Finally, he would take her away from that frenetic household to live a happy life with him.

But actually, as if things weren't bad enough, they got even worse when Papo turned thirteen. It was then that he had his first wet dream and began to fixate on the act of masturbation. One could hear him slapping away at himself and groaning with excitement at all hours of the day and night. He got to wacking off in the bathroom, the kitchen, the bedroom he shared with his parents, and, when he could sneak in, he even did it in Diedre's and Inez' room. As a matter of fact, there was not one inch of space in that apartment that Cousin Papo had not explored and used for his own sexual pleasure. Eventually Papo became so brazen that he began while at the dinner table. He would push back his chair, expose himself and pump away. Not even his mother's presence seemed to put him off. When ever this happened, cousin Diedre would scream out, "Mami . . . Mami, he's doing it again. Stop him!" At this, plump Aunt Ofelia would leap out of her chair, tripping as she rushed toward Papo who was grabbing at his penis. He would push her away with one hand while he continued to jerk away with the other.

"Papito . . . Stop! No, Papito, no . . . you mustn't do that! It's very bad. *Por Dios* . . . stop it now!" She would even go as far as to smack him. Finally, by leaning on him and using all of her strength, Aunt Ofelia would manage to get a hold of his small stiff organ that resembled a raw pork sausage link, push it into his pants and zip up his fly. While his mother, almost out of breath, tried to regain her composure, Papo would roll his eyes, throw back his head and laugh with delight.

"Disgusting, Mami. Simply gross! Why don't you beat him up? All you do is let him get away with it. You act like it's nothing!" Diedre would shout and begin to slap and punch her brother who by now was doubled up with laughter.

"Stop it . . .," Aunt Ofelia interfered, holding back her daughter. "He doesn't understand what he's doing. He's only a child. Papito will outgrow it if we leave him alone. Just ignore him. Don't look at him. Why are you always looking at him, eh?

You shouldn't be so interested in what your brother has in his pants. Look at her!" Aunt Ofelia would point to Inez, who all this time had sat quietly eating her food. "She's not even looking at him. Why don't you follow your cousin's example." Then Diedre would storm out of the room, screaming hysterically that she wanted to kill her brother.

Inez had seen this spectacle repeated many times before. She had no intention of becoming involved and so she behaved as if nothing unusual had happened. But in her thoughts, Inez fantasized killing them all. She imagined setting fire to the apartment, blocking the exits and trapping them into a slow and painful death. She thought of buying rat poison and putting it into Aunt Ofelia's beans and then watching everyone beg for mercy as she let them die, ignoring them just as she did now.

To make herself feel better, Inez would draw the most scathing caricatures of cousin Papo. Papo resembling his own penis, Papo eating his penis, or Papo as a rat with the body of a penis. The last one that had given Inez so much pleasure was a caricature of Cousin Diedre beating Papo to death with his penis.

One of the ways that Inez had managed to make her life bearable in that hostile environment was to take out a social security card as soon as she turned fourteen and get her working papers. Immediately afterward, she had found work as a page girl in the local public library. There she worked three evenings a week and all day Saturday, sorting out and storing books, pasting labels and doing anything else the librarians wanted done. For her labors she received a check every month. At the beginning, Aunt Ofelia demanded that she hand over her paycheck. Usually Inez was quietly stubborn, rebelling in passive ways, by not responding, not being on time or conveniently forgetting to do a chore or an errand. But this time she openly rebelled, yelling at her aunt.

"No! No way do you get my check. It's my money, I make it and I'll decide how to spend it. You don't touch it!" Aunt Ofelia thought better of challenging her strong-willed niece. Instead, she told Inez that for the privilege of handling her own money, she would now also be responsible for buying her own clothes and providing her own carfare and spending money. Never having had any other clothes except hand-me-downs and second-hand garments, and of course, never having seen any spending money except for the necessary carfare now and then, Inez happily accepted this arrangement.

From her meager earnings, Inez had not only managed to buy her own clothes (for now she had learned from her miserly aunt how to be a wise and thrifty shopper), but she had also saved enough to buy herself a large metal wardrobe with a strong pick-proof lock and key. Not for one moment did she trust her aunt or anyone else in that house. There, she kept all her worldly possessions, including old postcards, letters and photographs of her parents and brother, her drawing materials and, of course, all of her drawings.

Inez attended a local high school and was generally liked by her peers. The students and faculty especially praised her for her drawing and painting abilities. But because her aunt didn't permit her to remain after school to work on projects, nor was she allowed to bring friends home, her friendships were limited to the school grounds.

Aunt Ofelia watched both her daughter and niece like a hawk. Neither girl was allowed to date or to go out alone, unless she knew exactly where they went. Occasionally they would attend a church or school event in a mixed crowd of boys and girls, but usually they were discouraged and rarely participated in much of anything. Aunt Ofelia used their "bad" neighborhood as the major excuse, lecturing them on the wisdom of her actions.

"I'm telling you girls that Washington Heights has changed since the time we first moved here. Then you had decent hard-working Puerto Ricans, not all this riff-raff you got today . . . as well as those illegal aliens from Colombia and the Dominican Republic that come here pretending they are American citizens from Puerto Rico. There are too many muggings and rapes for you to go out alone. I don't want either one of you to associate with *basura* . . . that garbage out there they call humanity. And, I don't want you, under no circumstances, to mess around with any of those *titeres* . . . those bums that hang out on corners making obscene remarks at girls. You are both good Christians brought up properly and you will stay that way. This is a decent household and no shame is going to tarnish the Vasquez name."

Although there was some truth to the fact that Washington Heights was not the safest neighborhood in New York City, Aunt Ofelia had other reasons for behaving as she did toward the girls. Actually, she was always worried that her niece would meet some boy whom she would date in secret and eventually become pregnant. Then, not only would she have a double responsibility to deal with, but she could imagine what all the neighbors would say about her. As for her daughter, she wanted a rich professional son-in-law: a doctor or a lawyer. For this, she knew Diedre had to keep away from common folk, to go college and, of course, remain chaste.

However, in spite of all these restrictions, Inez had made two very good and close friends, Sheila Coleman and Loretta Sanchez. Both of these girls lived in the neighborhood, were in the same grade as Inez in the local high school and worked as page girls in the library. Sheila was a black girl who lived with her parents, four sisters and two brothers. Loretta was an only child who had come here from the Dominican Republic when she was three. She lived with her mother and stepfather. All three girls had become tight friends, confiding in each other. After graduation, Loretta was going to attend the University of Pennsylvania in Philadelphia where she would major in education. Sheila would work during the day and at night she would study accounting. When Inez told them that after graduation she would marry Joe Batista, they were upset.

"Come on girl . . .," Loretta responded "he's way too old for you. You don't even know him all that good . . . you only just met him a couple of months ago!"

"It's been three months . . . and I already know him pretty

well. Besides, he's not that old. He's just mature and more serious, not silly like some of the young guys . . . that's all."

"What about your plans for art school?" asked Sheila. "You should try to get a job after graduation and then move and go on to art school."

"But I am going to art school, after I get married. I already talked to Joe and he said it would be all right. Listen, you two would like him if you met him. He's very kind to me, always taking me out and treating me like I'm special. Honest."

"Well, I hope you're doing the right thing," Loretta said skeptically. "Marriage is pretty serious . . . and I just think you are too young. That's what I think."

"That's right, I'm still too young. I'm not even eighteen until January, and my aunt is in charge of me until I become twentyone. How am I gonna leave now? I mean, I'd have to get a job and save first to move out of there, and then save again to be able to study art. No . . . it will take too long that way. I can't stand it there any longer. I can't turn down this opportunity to finally leave . . .," she paused, then added, "the Vasquez house of horrors!" All three girls laughed.

"It looks to me like you already made up your mind," Sheila said.

"That's right," Inez nodded, "he's going to give me the ring soon and that will make it official."

"All right, then, you know I wish you the best of luck . . ." Loretta hugged her.

"Me too . . ." Sheila put her arms around Inez and kissed her on the cheek. "I'm happy if you are. We'll always be the best of friends."

"Inez was grateful to her friends. Throughout the years, Sheila and Loretta had been supportive and protective toward her. The many times when they knew Inez had come hungry to work at the library, they brought her food. Because Inez was never allowed to go to other peoples' homes, excuses had to be made up, such as working overtime, studying for an exam at the library and so on. Both Loretta and Sheila had gone as far as forging notes and making phone calls to Aunt Ofelia, pretending to be teachers or librarians, so that Inez could attend a birthday party or a special dinner at their homes.

"Don't forget too," Inez said, "you are both coming to the wedding. Promise?" They promised.

Part 2

Inez had met Joe Batista quite unexpectedly at a family gath-
ering. Aunt Ofelia rarely attended family celebrations of any
kind for fear of having to give money or a present.

"All they want is to get something out of me. Well, I'm not
giving them a thing," she would say.

However, for some odd reason, on this occasion — perhaps
she might have felt like socializing — Aunt Ofelia accepted the
invitation to attend the christening of Uncle Generoso's cousin
Luisa's baby daughter. She had even decided to bring along her
children, including Inez. Aunt Ofelia had opened the closet into
which she had jam-packed all the numerous articles she had
taken from her husband over the years, and after hours of
searching and deliberating, found a suitable gift. It was a genu-
ine down quilt made in Germany. Actually she already had about
six of these and reluctantly decided that she could part with one
of them.

After the church ceremony, while people were eating, drinking and milling about at Luisa's apartment, Joe Batista noticed
Inez and did not have eyes for anyone else but her. Inez was wearing a simple lavender cotton dress that fit snugly and smoothly
over her full firm breasts, small waist and generous hips. That
day she had put on the only jewelry she owned, which had been
left to her by her mother: earrings and a necklace of sparkling
garnets set in gold. Her long, straight, shiny brown hair hung
loosely over her shoulders. When she smiled at Joe, her straight
white teeth appeared like pearls against her dark pink lips.
When she walked, she seemed to radiate both an innocence and a
well-defined voluptuous sensuality. Joe was immediately smit-
ten by this young woman whom he had obviously never noticed
before. He engaged her in conversation, finding out as much as
he could about her. Finally, he asked her to go out with him.

"Maybe we can have dinner out and take in a movie." Joe

waited for her answer. But Inez was speechless — this was the first time a man had ever asked her for a date. "Look, Inez," Joe persisted, "we could do something else if you like. Whatever you want. You see, I'd like to take you out."

"Thank you . . .," Inez cleared her throat and spoke, overcoming her shyness at being approached by Joe, "but you see, you have to get my Aunt Ofelia's permission first. It's up to her."

"All right then. But if she says it's okay, will you let me take you out? We'll have a good time." Inez agreed, feeling her heart pounding and an excitement shaking her entire body.

When Joe Batista, elegible bachelor and a responsible citizen, showed an interest in her niece, Aunt Ofelia gladly gave him permission to date Inez. Even the remotest possibility that someone would take this stubborn girl off her hands, whom she considered a serious financial burden, was enough to make Aunt Ofelia leap for joy. With her blessings and encouragement, Joe and Inez began to date on a regular basis.

Aunt Ofelia's obsequious behavior toward Joe led him to take for granted his right to be with Inez almost every weekend. The couple went out to the movies, dinner and an occasional musical show. Aunt Ofelia's attitude toward Inez began to change; she spoke to her in a more courteous manner instead of just ordering her about. Also, Inez now found that her portions of food at dinner were more generous than usual. All the while, Aunt Ofelia never lost an opportunity to praise Uncle Generoso's third cousin.

"Why . . . that Joe is such a wonderful young man. And, he comes from a good home and a hardworking family. His father is Uncle Generoso's second cousin. You know, that woman he was married to was low life and that's why he divorced her. The story goes that he threw her out. After being married for three years, she was fooling around behind his back. Can you imagine? It was her loss. I mean, that Joe makes a wonderful salary and he goes to night school to study law . . . I'm telling you, he's a good catch for any girl."

After dating for two months, Joe invited Inez to meet his parents and family. Inez had sat in his parents' living room, trying not to feel self-conscious, as the elderly couple stared anxiously at her. They both expressed their wish that Joe would someday marry a young woman who would give them many grandchildren. Secretly, they hoped she would be the one . . . and that she was also going to save their son from the lonely life of an unattached bachelor. Nelida, Joe's single sister, two years his senior, had sat in an armchair sulking; this evening she felt old and homely, next to the young vivacious Inez, and she barely hid her resentment.

A month later, Joe presented Inez with an engagement ring. It had a small white diamond in the center with two diamond chips on either side.

"Even though I already asked you to marry me, here's the ring. Now we're officially engaged. I want to do right by you."

It's so beautiful!" Inez exclaimed as she watched the small diamond ring being placed on the third finger of her left hand. No one had ever given her such a grand present.

"Now you know I'm serious, baby." This time when he kissed her, he put his hand under her blouse and squeezed her breasts. Inez, had stiffened and drawn away. She had just gotten used to his tongue in her mouth and was even enjoying it, but this frightened her. "You have to let me do it . . . now we're engaged and it's my right." Obediently, Inez sat back and let him fondle, squeeze and kiss her breasts. "I won't go any further until we're married, because I know you're a virgin," he said.

Sometimes when Inez stopped to think about her commitment to marry Joe, she was filled with apprehension; everything was happening too quickly. She felt that in reality she had very little to say about anything. Joe was the one making all the decisions for them. She didn't know if she really loved him . . . after all, she had never gone out with anyone else. Joe had been the first man to ever kiss or touch her. But when these feelings began to overwhelm her, Inez would consider what the consequences would be if she didn't marry Joe. She would have to remain living in her present situation for who knew how long? The thought of getting away, leaving for good, pushed any doubts or fears from her mind. For now, all she wanted to do was escape as fast and as far away as she could.

After the official engagement, Inez began to confide in Joe. She told him about the way her Aunt mistreated her, about her hatred for the Vasquez family and about her need to get away from them. Joe always listened sympathetically, reassuring her that she wouldn't have that kind of life with him.

"They don't even have to set foot in our house, if you don't want it baby," he comforted her. Inez had put only one condition to him which she insisted upon before she would actually marry him. This was that they must not live in Washington Heights. Inez wanted to move as far away as possible from her Aunt.

"I'd like us to live in a better neighborhood too, where it's safer. I don't want to live in this area anymore, and I definitely don't want to be near my aunt." Because it had been the only condition she had set forth, and she had seemed so adamant in her request, Joe readily agreed.

However, when she spoke to him about her passion for art and her desire to go to art school, Joe was not as responsive; in fact, he appeared disinterested. She had proudly shown him her still-life sketches, her portraits and her landscapes, hoping for an enthusiastic reaction. Instead, he had simply nodded barely making a comment.

"Don't you like my work?" Inez asked.

"Hey . . . sure, I do. They are real nice. Very good. I think it's wonderful that you have this talent."

"Wait until after we get married and I begin to study. Then you'll really see what I can do." Joe had smiled as if he were amused with her. "I'm serious Joe, I want to study art. You must know that. It'll be all right, won't it?"

"Sure it will, baby. Sure," he had assured her, "whatever you want," before reaching over to squeeze her breasts and kiss her on the mouth.

Inez had been somewhat unsettled by Joe's laconic response and lack of interest in her artwork. Intuitively, she decided not to show him her caricatures of the Vasquez family. Inez was afraid Joe would disapprove. But she was also certain that after they were married, she could make him understand just how much studying art meant to her.

Except for this minor issue (which Inez felt she could handle), she was genuinely happy. Even her fantasies of committing murder against the Vasquez family faded. She now had happier thoughts to occupy her mind. Inez looked forward to graduating high school, getting married, going on her honeymoon and moving into her very own apartment . . . in exactly that order.

Joe kept his word and managed to rent an apartment out of the Washington Heights area in a good location on the upper West Side. It consisted of a large room with a modern kitchenette, a tiny foyer, bathroom and a medium-sized bedroom. As soon as he rented it, Joe moved in, bringing with him all the furniture that he had been keeping in storage from his previous marriage. The divorce settlement had given his ex-wife the car and property in upstate New York, while he had kept all the furniture. Joe was now quite pleased with himself: he was giving his new bride a fully furnished apartment; all she had to do was move in. It was all worth it for Inez, he had thought, she's a beautiful innocent girl . . . pure, a virgin. She was not like Ida, that fucking ex-wife of mine who fucked every pair of pants in Washington Heights . . . no sir, this one's a good girl, he had said to himself. The high rent he would have to pay every month upset him, until he remembered Inez. She's young and easy to train, he thought, I could get her to do things my way, never mind the rest . . . she's a good investment for my future.

By being thrifty, Inez had somehow, miraculously, managed to save from her pitiful earnings at the library, a total of one hundred and ten dollars. She had kept this money hidden away, tied inside a sock at the bottom of her metal wardrobe, under lock and key. Her plan had been to save enough so that one day she could leave. Now, she reasoned, she was in a way using the money for that purpose. With her savings she would buy her wedding outfit: a practical light blue suit with a white blouse and matching accessories. Except for the few new items she purchased, her trousseau was simply all the clothes she already owned.

Diedre, who at first had been more distraught and tearful than ever at the thought that Inez would be leaving her alone, was now cooperative and excited, since she had been chosen to be the maid of honor. Aunt Ofelia was so ecstatic, knowing that she would no longer have to feed or spend another penny on her niece, that she even offered to give the couple a reception at her apartment. The buffet luncheon would be her and Uncle Generoso's wedding gift to the couple. Another reason was that she felt someday she might be needing the services of Joseph Anthony Batista, Attorney at Law. It was best to stay on the good side of her niece and nephew.

"Inez, you are a very very lucky girl. Someday Joe Batista will be a lawyer and you will be a lawyer's wife. Do you have any idea how much money lawyers make? I could only wish the same good fortune for my Diedre. And to think I was the one that brought you two together. Remember that, even though you will be a married woman soon, you always have a home here with me."

Two days before the wedding, Inez packed all her belongings into a large old canvas suitcase, a duffle bag and two cardboard cartons. Joe borrowed a car and transported them to their new apartment. Inez sold her metal wardrobe to Diedre for twenty dollars, complete with pick-proof lock and key. She had carefully packed all her caricatures in between two pieces of cardboard and tightly sealed them. Later, she gave them to Sheila to store them for her at her house, along with some other drawings. Inez counted all the money she had left: twenty dollars and seventy one cents.

The brief ceremony was held at the rectory of the neighborhood Catholic church. Uncle Generoso gave the bride away; Freddy Martinez, Joe's oldest friend and best man produced the rings on cue; and Cousin Diedre, dressed all in pink as the maid of honor, kept her promise and sobbed in a subdued manner, never once becoming hysterical. Inez repeated her vows without much emotion or commitment; all that these words meant to her was a passport to freedom. Joe had kissed her passionately after the ceremony, whispering in her ear, "This time it's for keeps, baby . . ." Inez had smiled at him, not fully comprehending what he meant.

To Inez' astonishment, Aunt Ofelia had ample food and drink, including a small wedding cake. Even cousin Papo dressed up in a suit and tie and behaved — he had heeded his mother's warning after a five dollar bribe. Not once did he open his fly or play with himself. Except for Loretta and Sheila, the best man and his wife Lucy, only the immediate family attended the reception. All in all, everyone had a pleasant time.

That night back at their new apartment, Joe made love to Inez twice and each time he was eager, greedy and quick. When he first approached her, Inez had been dumbfounded and frightened at the full size of his penis, since all she had ever seen close up was Papo's adolescent "pork sausage." Then she had also felt awkward, not really knowing what to do with her arms and legs. She had lain back submissively, experiencing pain instead of pleasure. When, finally, Joe finished, rolled over and fell asleep, Inez felt an enormous sense of relief. A sharp piercing pain shot through her legs up into her vagina and further into her insides. Inez got up and quietly limped to the bathroom. Reaching down, she wiped her hand against the sticky wetness of her crotch and jumped back in fear as she saw the mixture of blood and semen. Even though Sheila had warned her that she might bleed the first time she had sex — "My older sister Charlene told me you bleed at the beginning until you get used to doing it" — Inez was still scared and upset. She took a washcloth and carefully and gently cleaned herself with warm water; then she found her way back to bed. Inez prayed that it wouldn't be this painful every time they made love. She concentrated on tomorrow, the plane ride and the honeymoon in Miami Beach . . . only good thoughts. Yet it would be hours before she could fall asleep.

The next morning, Joe picked up the sheets and carefully examined the blood stains.

"Ah ha! Baby, I knew it for sure. You were a virgin all right . . . you weren't fooling me. But no more! I got you now. Now, baby, you are mine!" he grinned, pleased with himself, and he reached over to Inez and kissed her on the navel.

"No, please!" Inez withdrew.

"Okay," he said, "it's all right. Are you sore, honey?"

"Yes," she whispered. "Please not now . . ."

"Sure . . . I'll leave you alone. We'll do it tonight. And next time, I'll be gentler, I promise. I'll do it real easy." After Joe finished his shower, Inez filled the tub with hot water and soaked herself for a long time. Feeling better, she began to get ready for the honeymoon and life as a married woman.

Part 3

"All right, Inez, this will be the long pose. Sit here. That's right . . . next to the still life. Turn your head a little more to the left, eyes downcast, fold your hands thus. That's it, perfect! The instructor then set the stop watch for twenty-five minutes and turned to address his students.

"This is the pose the model will hold for the next four sessions. There will be two more of these long poses for this evening. Okay, everybody begin."

Inez sat perfectly still posing in the large studio, oblivious to the twenty-odd art students as they sketched or painted with their eyes focused on her nakedness in order to capture a likeness. As a student here herself, she knew what it was to be on the other side of the room, facing a naked model. It meant hard work and the power to concentrate on the varied and complex lines, shapes, planes and shadows of the face and body in order to learn anatomy and translate it into a good final drawing or painting. Inez had been attending evening classes at the Art Students League on West 57th Street for four months. She had been posing as a nude model for nearly two months out of the four.

With her eyes downcast, Inez focused on the toes of her left foot. She had discovered that if she relaxed into the pose, then used this time to think and try to sort out some of her problems, she would be less tired at the end of class. Her problems centered around Joe Batista, who was now her nemesis. She would console herself with the thought that Joe was only one person, compared to her former keepers, an entire family. Somehow she had managed to get away from "them" and somehow she vowed to get away from "him."

In the meantime, she had been cunning and clever. Joe knew nothing about her lessons, nor her part-time job as a nude model at the League. At times she wondered just what Joe would do if he found out that she was not only taking art lessons, but posing

naked in a room full of strangers . . . many of whom were men.
When this thought crossed her mind, Inez would experience a
wide range of feelings, from wanting to burst out laughing to
hiding, to shaking with fear at the thought of facing Joe. Joe
Batista was insanely jealous, possessed of a nasty temper and
easily provoked to violence.

The first time that Inez had clearly seen this violent side of her
husband's character was when she had fallen ill. Shortly after
they were married, Ines had gotten the flu and could barely
move. She asked Joe to call the seventy-four-year-old Dr. Gon-
salvo Marcos-Prieto, who had been attending the Vasquez family and everyone else in her old neighborhood for what seemed
to be forever.

"You what? You want me to call who?" he had screamed at
her. "You aint going to see that old lecher. I don't want him looking at you or touching you . . . understand?"

"But he's always been my doctor," Inez protested.

"Not any more. I know that old sucker, Marcos-Prieto, and
he likes to feel young ass. You're not going there . . . no way!"
When Inez tried to defend the old doctor, Joe had kicked the
night table across the room and flung the pillows into the air
punching them. "No! *Coño!* I'm gonna get you a woman doctor.
I'll find one right now. You are never going to that old prick
again." Inez had silently watched Joe as he searched through the
yellow pages, making phone calls and inquiries. Finally he
found a female physician who had her practice nearby. Joe's
choice ironically turned out to be a great help to Inez. Had he
known the results of her subsequent visits to this woman, he
would have undoubtedly gone into one of his murderous rages.

Dr. Helen McCarthy was a young internist and an intensely
avid feminist who lost very little time in acquainting Inez with
the various methods of birth control. After assessing Inez' situation, Dr. McCarthy decided to fit her with an Inter Uterine
Device.

"Never mind that he doesn't approve of your using any birth

control. I don't want to hear any more about his tyrannical philosophy. You are not even eighteen years of age! Do you want to become pregnant before you even have a chance to know what life is all about? Do you? Then what happens to all your plans to study art? Besides, I really do not believe that you want to have children with a bully like Joe Batista. And please, don't tell me about how he takes precautions by wearing condoms and pulling out before ejaculation. That's exactly how dumb females like yourself get pregnant! It's your body, young lady, and your vagina . . . and you must take care of yourself. Understood! Now, you might bleed a little when I first put in the I.U.D. You are not to worry about this. Come back and I'll check it out and readjust it if necessary. In time, I guarantee you will become used to this method and won't feel a thing. Also, the bleeding will stop. Don't say a word to your husband . . . pretend your periods are uneven, and he will be none the wiser. Keep checking in with me until you feel you are okay."

And so it was to be, because Inez did exactly as Dr. McCarthy instructed her, and Joe was never to find out about her personal birth control method.

This secret triumph gave Inez the strength to fight back and win yet another battle that was very important in her struggle for independence. The second time Joe displayed violence toward Inez, she not only confronted his authority, but fought back. After graduation and her honeymoon, Inez at age seventeen-and-a-half, had entered the job market with virtually no skills. Her majors in high school, English and art (she couldn't even type) prepared her for very little except the most menial of jobs. However, because she was pretty and had a pleasant personality, she was able to find steady employment as a receptionist-file clerk at minimum wage with an insurance brokerage firm. When Inez brought her first paycheck home — just as had happened before with Aunt Ofelia — Joe wanted Inez to give him her wages. She refused, reminding him that she preferred to handle her own money so that she could save for her enrollment in art school.

"Remember, I told you how I planned to study art as soon as I could save so that I . . ."

"Forget about all this art school bullshit!" Joe interrupted. "Me! The man . . . the macho of the house. I have my law degree to get, remember? And that takes money. I have to pay for all my credits, books, everything!"

"But, I thought you understood about my going to art school, and . . ."

"Crap, *mierda* . . ." Joe went into a temper tantrum screaming and kicking furniture. "Fuck your art school! Isn't it enough that I'm stuck with this apartment that you had to have — in a better neighborhood away from your Aunt Ofelia — which is costing me an arm and a leg. I have to pay this fucking high rent every month, and now I need your paycheck. That's all there is to it! You have to contribute, baby, bring in some bucks. I don't even have a car because that bitch of an excuse for a woman I was married to took it from me. All right, I'll manage . . . and I'll live out of Washington Heights, right here where you like it so much better! I won't even complain about the expensive honeymoon I took you on. Remember? A whole week in Miami Beach? Then, there's the ring I bought you too. You didn't bring a fucking penny with you into this marriage. You came to me with nothing, baby. Nothing! A fucking orphan is what I married. Now you got yourself a fully furnished apartment, clothes, a job, a husband . . . now, what the hell more do you want? No way, art school. No way! You can paint your little flowers and still-lifes right here. You don't need school for the shit you do. Use the entire apartment and make believe it's art school. I'm never here to interfere, because I'm working my ass off and then going to night school. So . . . you just amuse yourself at home, and cut out this art school shit!" Joe picked up a chair and flung it across the room. "Listen, bitch, hand over that check every week . . . just like I have to use all my earnings to pay for all this shit here. You just come on and fucking do the same."

Inez was stunned by Joe's words, because even though she knew that he had never been supportive or particularly interested in her art work, she had not expected him to forbid her to go to art school. As she watched Joe rant and rave, overturning chairs, tossing papers and books about the room, Inez remembered that she had been through this before and even worse. Memories of her Aunt's punishments, cousin Papo's willfullness, cousin Diedre's hysterics and all those years of abuse she had managed to survive, rushed into her mind, and at that moment she lost all fear of what Joe might do to her.

"I'm not giving you my paycheck!" Inez screamed. "My Aunt tried and she couldn't take it away from me either. I work for what's mine and I keep it . . . you're not getting it!" Joe stopped amazed and disarmed by Inez' response. They stared at each other silently, as if they were in a boxing arena. Then Joe gritted his teeth, clenched his fists and started toward Inez. Quickly she jumped back.

"Keep away! Keep away from me! Don't you touch me, you bastard. I'll fucking kill you, I will. You don't lay a hand on me!" Inez grabbed a large flat cast iron grill that hung on a peg board in the kitchenette. She held it by the handle with both hands, as if it were a tennis racket she was ready to swing, and stood squarely with both feet apart facing him. He stood before her with his eyes and mouth wide open. Inez could hear her own heavy breathing as she cautiously eyed him, ready to bash him if he so much as came near her. Joe retreated a few paces very carefully holding up both hands in a gesture of surrender, indicating that he was now calm and wanted a peaceful solution.

"Hey . . .," he spoke softly, "what are you doing, baby? I wasn't gonna hit you. Honest, come on take it easy. You don't have to do this to me. I only want to make a better life for the both of us. I swear, honest. Come on sweetheart." He took a step toward Inez and immediately she held up the grill ready to strike him. "Hey! You might as well stop this, because I'm not going to hurt you. All I want is for us to talk . . . I swear it. *Te lo juro,*

Mami! I love you, baby, and I wouldn't hurt you for the whole world. I may lose my temper, but that don't mean I'll harm you. Baby, I want us to be together forever . . . I want us to have kids and everything. Come on . . . please. Please . . ." Slowly Joe began to pick up the books and papers he had strewn about the room; he put the chairs and all the other furniture back in place. "See?" he shrugged. "Truce, Inez, okay?" Calmly Inez hung the grill back on it's hook, folded her hands and stood waiting. "That's more like it. Let's talk, honey. What do you say?" he pleaded.

"I'll give you my share toward the house, Joe." Inez spoke in a steady voice, "but I keep my paycheck and handle my earnings."

"All right! That's it . . . honey. That's all I want." Joe said relieved, "Now we can work something out."

The final agreement was that Inez would contribute half of all her earnings to household expenses. With the other half, she would have to meet her own needs: carfare, lunch, clothes and whatever else she needed. Actually, she felt the settlement was not so terrible, after all. She was now making a lot more money than she had as a page girl in the library. She was also confident that she could save for art school and somehow manage on her salary.

Joe had become so sexually stimulated by their fight, that when he made love to her that night, he was almost like a madman wanting to devour her. But this time it was different for Inez. She became assertive, letting him know what she did not like and what she wanted. And, for the first time since she had been having sex with her husband, she experienced an orgasm. The next morning, Inez awoke feeling a sensation of tranquility and contentment extending throughout her entire body. She yawned, sat up and looked over at Joe. Inez studied him as he lay on his stomach with his head turned to the right, his mouth slightly parted and emiting a soft snore. She decided that she definitely did not love him.

"Time . . . Inez, you can take your break now." She heard the instructor's voice as the buzzer on the stop watch sounded. "Ten minutes, everyone," he called out. Inez stood and stretched, feeling the circulation coming back into her limbs. Then she went behind the screen, put on her robe and sandals, grabbed her purse and went out of the studio into the foyer. She found the soft drink machine, inserted some change in the slot and selected an orange drink.

"Hi, Inez!" she turned and saw Aldo Fanelli.

"You working tonight?" he asked.

"Yes. How are you?"

"Great. Listen, after you finish working, why don't you come out with some of us to Charlie's for a drink?"

"Thanks, but I have to get home early tonight."

"Okay . . . but how long can you keep on saying no? When are you going to let me treat you to a beer?"

"I told you Aldo, I don't drink."

"How about a coke . . . or a cup of coffee, then? I'm buying."

"All right, soon." Inez smiled at him, "one evening when I can stay late. I promise."

"Now I heard you say that 'you promised,' so I'm holding you to it. Look, I've got to get back to class. You take care, Inez."

Inez watched as he waved, turned and walked back into one of the studios. She had liked Aldo immediately. He was the instructors's assistant in the very first class she had attended. Aldo was warm and friendly, showing her around the League, introducing her to people and he even helped her select the art equipment she needed. Although she considered him a friend, she never spoke to him about her personal life. He, as well as the other students, knew very little about Inez, except for the fact that she was also aspiring to be an artist, just like the rest of them. When she had registered at the Art Students League, Inez had given Sheila Coleman's address and phone number, so that no one would know where she lived. Sheila had been supportive when she found out Inez was ready to study.

"Don't you worry about Joe finding out," she had said, "just go ahead and give my address and phone number. I'll tell my folks, just in case you get mail or phone calls. You know they won't ask questions . . . they'll accept whatever I tell them." Inez knew she was right; Sheila had a very loving family. Besides they knew Inez' past and had always treated her well. She felt safe in doing this.

When people at the League saw her wedding band and asked her about her husband, she told them he was away in the air force. Then she would change the conversation, discouraging any more talk or questions concerning her personal life. Some of her classmates thought she was stuck-up. Aldo would always come to her defense.

"No, it has nothing to do with her being stuck-up. I think Inez has her own personal reasons for not hanging out. Also, she's a very private person." Most of them pretended to accept his argument because they could see he was quite taken with Inez and would defend her, no matter what the truth was.

The money that Inez had saved from her wages began to run out after almost two months of study at the league. When she was faced with the reality of not being able to continue classes, she spoke to Aldo.

"Why don't you work as a model here? It's a good chance they'll take you. They already know you. Look, you don't have to know anything, how to type or do bookkeeping . . . all you have to do is take off your clothes and sit still. They pay the minimum wage, just like any place else. I'll bet you can get the hours you want. I do it from time to time when I'm short of money . . . it's very easy."

The idea of taking off all her clothes before strangers horrified Inez. She tried first asking for a raise and for overtime at work. When both requests were refused, Inez decided that she would do anything in order to continue her studies. Her voluptuous body and dark features made her a very interesting subject. But she could also hold her poses without fidgeting or falling asleep. Soon her reputation as a good model got her more hours than she could handle.

Inez finished her orange soda and went back into the studio. Once again, she sat relaxing into the pose. She thought about her work at the League and wondered just how long she could keep on going like this. She was living from day to day, not knowing exactly where she was heading. The future seemed like some mysterious puzzle that, at least for now, she couldn't deal with. For the time being, she was happy accepting things as they were. Fortunately, Joe was always busy with working overtime and attending night classes four times a week. This had enabled Inez to work as a model two nights a week and attend classes the other two nights . . . all right on schedule with Joe. The money she earned as a part-time model paid for her courses and art supplies.

Joe, of course, had no idea as to what his wife did with her evenings when he was gone. Since she contributed her fair share of money every week and never complained, he assumed she was happy watching television or amusing herself working on her little pictures. Inez had cleverly set herself up in a corner of the living room with a small table containing inks, pastels and oil paints. There she had sketches and small canvasses of flowers, still-lifes and animal portraits. In this way, not only would Joe think she was working at home, but he would get used to the smell of linseed oil and turpentine which by now permeated most of her clothes. Except for mild curiosity on occasion, Joe rarely looked at her work. As far as he was concerned, things were going quite well between them.

Actually, Inez and Joe seldom saw each other. Whenever Joe had a free Friday night, he would always go out with "the guys." Weekends, when he wasn't studying for an exam, they might have dinner with his parents, go to a movie or visit Joe's best friend Freddy and his wife Lucy. Inez would use her spare time to clean up the apartment, read and practice sketching. Upon her insistence, they never saw the Vasquez family. She declined any offers Aunt Ofelia made, inviting them for dinner or a casual visit. When Diedre telephoned, Inez would promise that she would have her over when they were less busy. Actually, she had no intensions of ever seeing her again; as far as Inez was concerned, the Vasquez family was out of her life for good.

As a couple, Inez and Joe led a dull and uneventful life. But the world that Inez had constructed for herself was another matter. When she opened her eyes each morning, Inez was motivated to get through her day in order to arrive at the Art Students League. She was not quite cognizant of the reality she had worked so hard to develop, which had to do with her art work, her instructor and the people she knew, worked and studied with at the League. In no way did this world include her marriage and Joe Batista.

As the weeks became months. Inez found that she detested her husband. She resented his constant complaining about money and the way he scrutinized the supermarket receipts. Joe made her account for every penny she spent, chastising her whenever he could.

"What's this dollar and seventy cents for? We don't need to buy raisins or dried fruits . . . I don't eat that shit. And you have your face cream and shampoo on this bill. I thought we agreed you were supposed to pay for that stuff out of your money. In the future, don't be buying your personal crap out of the house money. Now, I expect you to make up for these two items, you hear?"

She found his greediness extended even to their lovemaking. He always wanted to have sex his way. Joe insisted on selecting the position, the length of foreplay and always expected Inez to be willing and ready whenever he wanted to have sex. She had discovered that the only way she could tolerate him and even enjoy herself, so that she would not be the passive recipient of her husband's lustful desires, was to fantasize about other men. In bed, Inez pretended that Joe was someone she had seen on the street, someone at work or at the League, even a celebrity in the movies or on television; almost any other man would do. More often than not, this technique worked for her.

In spite of having to share part of her life with a man she now genuinely loathed, Inez was not totally unhappy. She had her work, which by now had so greatly improved that her instructor was compelled to speak to her about her future. He had already chosen four of her drawings to be included in a school exhibit of works by a few selected students, and felt she had tremendous potential.

"You should try to study full time, I think you might try applying for a scholarship," Nat Ackerman had said to Inez. "You have done extremely well in the short time since you've been here. I can imagine how much better you would do if you had enough time to work and study. I'm sure you will qualify. There are a few good schools out of state, but I prefer the ones right here in the city. There is Pratt . . . N.Y.U. has a good art department and, of course, Cooper Union . . . but there are other schools, as well. I tell you what, I'll be happy to get you the information. You can check it out. I'll do everything I can to help you, Inez."

When he first spoke to Inez, such a possibility seemed to her to be beyond her reach . . . outside of the realm of her world. But Nat Ackerman had seemed so sure and was so encouraging that she was now ready to consider his advice.

"Time, Inez," she heard the instructor's voice and the buzzer. Inez took her second break, ate the supper she had brought with her: a hard-boiled egg, a cup of strawberry yogurt and an apple. That evening she finished her third pose, got dressed and headed for home, making sure she would get there before 11 P.M., that is, before Joe. She had synchronized her schedule down to the last minute so that all was going right on schedule. Although lately, Inez was becoming less anxious about getting home before Joe. Two days earlier, she had brought home some art literature and forgotten to put it out of sight. Luckily, she had arisen early, before Joe had found the brochures and newsletters where she had left them on one of the bookshelves. She was positive he hadn't even noticed them.

Part 4

That very evening, when Joe's Wednesday-night classes were cancelled because of student protests and demonstrations, was the same night Inez decided to stay later and have that drink with Aldo Fanelli.

Instead of being greeted by his wife, as he was expecting, Joe walked into a dark and empty apartment. He looked around for traces of Inez. She was not sleeping; she just wasn't there. Confused, he called out to her, "Inez, Inez, are you home?" He waited several moments in silence for her response, until he realized that she hadn't come home yet.

Joe tried to figure out where she might be. Perhaps she'd gone shopping, he thought; but then he remembered that she had very little money and the rule was that they always discussed whether any shopping had to be done. She's gone to see a friend, he said to himself.

"What friend?" he whispered. Except for Loretta and Sheila, Inez had no friends. Loretta wasn't even in the city anymore; she was going to some school in Pennsylvania. Joe knew how much Inez hated to go uptown to the old neighborhood where Sheila lived. Still, that was the only logical explanation, he reasoned, then decided to wait before calling Sheila. After all, Joe said to himself, she might get home any minute. He heated the soup that Inez had prepared and left on the stove for him, fixed himself a sandwich and opened up a can of beer.

After finishing his third beer, Joe checked the time; it was getting pretty late. When he was about to telephone Sheila, Joe remembered that just the other morning he had seen some pamphlets . . . they were on one of the bookshelves. At that time, he had glanced briefly at them, hardly noticing what they were about. Now he remembered that they were art brochures and newsletters. That's right, he recalled, the stuff had to do with a place . . . some school called the League of Student Artists, or

some such name, located on West 57th Street. Quickly Joe
looked all over the bookshelves and then inside the kitchen cabi-
nets, hoping to find the pamphlets. He searched among Inez'
drawings and art supplis, but found nothing.

"Where could that stuff be?" he shouted. "I know I saw those
pamphlets. Ah-ha . . . wait!" Joe went into the bedroom and
looked inside drawers and closets. "What did she do with that
crap? She's hiding something from me. I know it!" Exasper-
ated, Joe kicked a chair clear across the living room. "What the
hell is going on here, anyway?"

Inez sat at a booth in Charlie's Tavern sipping a gingerale and
being dazzled by Aldo Fanelli's charm as he related his life story.
After graduating from the University of Buffalo, three years
ago, Aldo had come to New York to pursue an art career. Now at
age twenty-five, he had his own loft on Canal Street, which
served as living quarters and studio. He had done a variety of
jobs while waiting to become a famous artist: messenger, sales-
man, stock boy, house painter and model at the league.

"My whole family still lives in Buffalo. They were all upset
when I left for New York. Especially my father . . . he freaked
out. You know what his last words to me were? 'You, the first one
in the family to go to college, eh? And you get a degree to starve?
Hey Leonardo Da Vinci, how you gonna live? You gonna eat
your paintings?' He wanted me to go into the family business.
Repairing and putting on roofs . . . a nice steady job. I should
carry on just like my brothers and cousins. Everybody is con-
nected to the family business. You gotta understand, Inez, my
family is typically Italian," Aldo interlocked his fingers and held
up his hands, "like this, inseparable! They all have to work
together, live together, eat together and die together. Man, give
me a break! I had to get out of there. Of course, they all think I've
got a screw loose for leaving, coming to New York and wanting
to be an artist. But," Aldo shrugged, "I don't care. If I had
stayed in Buffalo, I'd of really gone crazy."

"Do you ever miss them?" she asked.

"No. But sometimes I think of my sister Lorraine. She's older than me . . . but we were close. Lorraine's very sensitive. In fact, she's about the only one in my family that's been to a museum and has any interest in art. But other than Lorraine, I don't miss them at all. I'm happy to be here in New York, where I can be in contact with other artists and exhibit my work. Speaking of which . . . you know what? The Wildemina Gallery in Soho . . . you know the one that has put my work in two group shows? They may take me on as a regular . . . that means I might get a one-man show next year!"

"That's wonderful, Aldo." Inez sat back feeling quite content, waiting to hear more.

"Okay, now that's enough about me, I've been talking too much. Let's hear something about your life. Come on, mystery woman . . . what about you?"

"Mystery woman, me?" Inez was surprised, she couldn't believe anyone would call her that.

"Sure. You never say a word about yourself. All we know is that you appear at the League and then vanish. Tell us about your secret life."

Inez didn't know what to say. She never suspected that Aldo or any of the other students were curious about her.

"Come on, pretty lady," Aldo spread out his arms and pretended to plead, "please tell papa who you really are. I promise I won't tell another soul!"

Inez laughed enjoying everything about him, his demonstrative way of speaking, the way he tilted his head when he smiled, even the way he walked with a quick lithe step. She realized that she was very attracted and drawn to Aldo and began to blush with embarrassment.

"Hey, wait a minute." He could see she was uncomfortable. "You don't have to tell me a thing, honest. I was only joking. I'm just happy to be here sitting with you." He reached over and touched her hand. Quickly she withdrew, feeling as if she were burning up. "Relax, honest, I'm not trying to pry. I just want to be your friend. Let's change the subject, if you want."

"No," Inez said regaining her composure. "There just isn't much to tell, really. I was born in New York City. My parents died when I was little. My father died when I was five and my mother when I was eleven. They had come here from Puerto Rico. Anyway, after that, my aunt raised me. I lived with her and her family, my cousins and uncle, until I graduated high school. Then I got married and moved out."

"Whew!" Aldo said, "hold on . . . you just told me your whole life story in a few sentences. How long ago was all that? Like, when did you graduate? What did you do after that? And when did you get married?"

"Oh, almost eleven months ago. I graduated last June and got married that same week."

"How old are you, anyway?"

"Eighteen."

"Eighteen! Holy shit! I didn't know you were so young. You're just a kid." Inez frowned at him, feeling disappointed. "No . . . it's okay, I didn't mean it the way it sounded. I'm sorry. What I meant is that you act much more mature than some of the older chicks I know. Really, that's why I thought you were close to my age. It's cool, really. How about a smile? You're not gonna stay mad at me, are you?" Inez smiled at him. "That's better. Now, what about your old man . . . your husband? What's he do?"

"Oh, he's in the air force. He's a corporal stationed in Fort Bragg, North Carolina." Inez gave her brother Frankie's last address. She felt uncomfortable having to lie to Aldo and averted her eyes. At this moment she would have liked to tell him the truth about Joe and her life.

"Do you still live with your aunt . . . I mean, since your husband's not around . . ."

"No. Absolutely not. I never liked her or her family. We didn't get along. I live . . . I live with my best girlfriend Sheila Coleman and her family. But that's only temporary until my husband gets his discharge."

"When is he getting out of the service?"

"Oh . . ." Inez paused, "well, we're not sure just yet. He hasn't decided."

"Do you ever get to see him much?"

"Of course I do . . . I mean as much as I can under the circumstances. He comes home on furlough and, of course, he writes to me every single day and calls me long distance very often. He cares a lot about me, you know."

"What's his name?"

"Frankie . . . his name is Frankie."

"Well, that Frankie is a very lucky guy to have someone like you. I'd do the same if I were your old man. In fact, I'd be afraid to leave you alone."

"He doesn't have to worry," Inez looked directly at Aldo, "you see, I love him very much too."

"Like I said, he's a lucky man."

"I'm lucky too because Frankie understood I wanted to study art and he encouraged me. That's why I'm here in New York instead of in North Carolina with him."

"Your work is good, Inez. Very good. Everybody knows it too. You should try to go even further with your art."

"You know what? That's what my instructor Nat Ackerman said. Look, he's just given me all this material," Inez reached into her bag, "a bunch of brochures and applications. All of this." She spread the literature out on the table. "He wants me to try for a scholarship so that I can study full time."

"I think it's a great idea!"

"You do? Oh Aldo, I'd like to try."

"Then do it, try. Let me look at this stuff . . ." Aldo examined the applications. "Look, I'll help you fill out all of this stuff, if you want. And, I'll help you prepare for any exams you might have to take. I'm good at that shit . . . I know what they expect. That's why I always got top grades in school."

"Oh, thank you so much. I really appreciate it. Nat Ackerman said he would help me too . . . as much as he could."

"Definitely try for Cooper Union. That would be my first choice. It's one of the best schools in the city and they give you a very good deal. Besides, that way you won't have to leave New York."

"I will." She smiled gratefully at Aldo. "Thank you."

"Tell me, what made you want to study art, Inez? Like, when did you know you wanted to be an artist?"

"Always. Ever since I can remember. In fact, I don't remember wanting to be anything else but an artist. When I was real little, I used to make drawings of everything and everyone I saw. My mother used to tell me I had talent. She said God had blessed me in that way."

"Me too!" Aldo said. "My older sister Lorraine said the same thing to me, and she used to buy paper and crayons so I could draw. She was the only one who really encouraged me. Inez, we have so much in common. You know what I believe? I think that being an artist is something that a person is born with . . . and you and I are born artists." They continued to share feelings about their work. For the first time in her life Inez felt that someone really understood what it was she was saying, and cared.

Inez checked the large clock on the wall. "Oh my God, it's late!" She jumped up. "I have to go."

"I'll take you home. It's too late for you to ride on the subways alone."

"No! You musn't!" Inez spoke so firmly and looked so upset that Aldo was startled by her reaction. "I mean, thank you . . . but I'll be just fine. I don't live all that far."

"Are you sure? Look, Inez, are you all right?"

"Yes, please, I'm fine."

Aldo walked Inez to the subway and, before they parted, he got her to promise she would see him again very soon so that they could work on the applications. Inez looked at her wristwatch impatiently. If the train was on time, she wouldn't be late, otherwise she was cutting it close. Luckily, her train arrived promptly. Tonight Joe was usually home by about twelve-thirty to one o'clock. It was only a few minutes past midnight when Inez turned the key, opened the door and walked into a dark apartment, confident that she would have time to wash and get to bed before Joe. Instead, her heart almost stopped beating when she switched on the light and saw the dirty dishes in the sink, three empty beer cans on the table and an overturned chair. Swiftly and barely making a sound, she took the literature out of her bag and put everything safely away in a plastic shopping bag she had hidden behind the drain pipes in the kitchen cabinet under the sink. There she kept all the literature she had about the League, information on current art exhibits, art newsletters, as well as the pay stubs from her modeling job. Then, very carefully she tiptoed over to the bedroom and peeked in. Sure enough, there was Joe sleeping soundly.

Inez went back to the living room feeling slightly nauseous. What awful luck, she thought, this was the first time in over four months that she had decided to stay late and Joe had to come home unexpectedly. She had to sort this out before tomorrow. What could she tell him? How could she explain where she was tonight? Had Joe telephoned Sheila's house? She could say that she had been shopping . . . no that wouldn't do, after all, she had bought nothing. If he had called Sheila, he'd know she wasn't there. Think . . . Inez said to herself, think . . . all right, overtime. That's it, she had been working overtime. Tomorrow she'd speak to Mary MacDonald, her supervisor. She'd figure something out by morning. Inez' head was spinning as she very quietly washed up, undressed and slipped into her side of the bed turning her back to him. She pretended to fall asleep immediately. Inez lay motionless and tense anticipating that Joe might wake up, start a row or reach out and want to make love. To her relief, he did not stir nor make a sound, in fact, he seemed to be sleeping quite peacefully.

The next morning when Joe confronted her, Inez told him that there was a lot of overtime at work.

"I figured I could make some extra money and I decided you wouldn't mind."

"Okay, baby. I hope to see some of them extra bucks coming this way." Joe stood very close to Inez with his hands clenched at his sides, grinning and staring silently at her. She shrank away from him, retreating several steps. "It's all right, honey . . . I'm not gonna harm you. Just be careful coming home late on the subway. The boogey man might get you and I don't want my little girl getting hurt."

The next day it took every ounce of courage she had to speak to her supervisor. Inez tried not to falter as she explained how important art school was to her and about Joe's attitude.

"You see Mrs. MacDonald, my husband is kind of old-fashioned. But, all I want to do is study art. So in case he should call you . . ."

"It's okay, honey . . .," chubby Mary MacDonald winked at Inez, "you don't have to make up any stories on my account. I've been there myself. If you got a boyfriend on the side, it doesn't matter to me."

"No, wait, you don't understand . . ." At first Inez tried to clarify her situation, but her supervisor wasn't interested.

"I said it's all right, honey."

"Thank you," Inez replied, deciding it didn't really matter.

When Inez telephoned Sheila, she was relieved to hear that Joe had not called there. Inez told Sheila that she was applying for scholarships to several art schools and that she would be expecting replies within the next few weeks.

"Check the mail for me, and if anything comes, telephone me right away. Please."

"Don't you worry, Inez, I'll call you first thing. In the mean-time, be careful and if you need me, let me know." Like always, Sheila was a good friend.

Now, each and every day before Inez went to the League, she would first telephone St. John's University to make sure that

Joe's classes were definitely being given that evening. After she had handed him an extra twenty dollars, Joe had not asked any more questions nor pressed her further. He never mentioned that night again and seemed to act normally: totally self-involved and not the least bit interested in her art work. Two weeks passed before Inez could feel relaxed and secure that all was going smoothly once more.

As for Joe, he routinely began to telephone the apartment evenings when he was at school. Sometimes he called three and four times a night . . . his calls were never answered. Joe had also called her office during the evening and there had been no answer as well. Now he was definitely convinced that Inez was doing something behind his back. Was she just going to art school . . . he wondered. Or, was she seeing another man? After all, he telephoned her four nights a week and she was never home. How could she afford to take courses and buy art supplies? Something was just too strange here. Even though he was becoming more and more enraged with Inez, Joe had decided not to panic. He would stay cool, not call Sheila, who most likely would lie for Inez, nor would he call her supervisor either. In fact, he didn't want to arouse Inez' suspicions that he was on to her. No, instead he would wait until he could take an evening off from school and simply follow her. He'd catch her at whatever she was doing. In the meantime, he had searched the entire apartment from top to bottom and found nothing that could incriminate her. Then, one day quite by accident as he was looking for the bottle of suede shoe polish, Joe found her plastic shopping bag stuffed with all kinds of papers. He examined everything in the bag, becoming livid with anger when he saw the applications and Sheila Coleman's return address. When he found her pay stubs, he put two and two together. So that's how she pays for her courses and supplies, he thought, she works at the League, probably as a clerk or receptionist. Angrily, Joe put everything back in the shopping bag and replaced it behind the pipes. All right, he was now determined to get to the bottom of

all of this and find out what the fuck Inez was doing behind his
back . . . the bitch!

The following week Inez sat in her long pose. Her mind was
filled with expectations and hope that one of the several schools
she had applied to would reply with some good news. She had
sent transcripts of her high school records, samples of her work
and letters of recommendation. She had also stated that she was
prepared to work part-time in order to help pay for her tuition.
What she tried not to think about, but could not put out of her
mind, was what she would do if she were accepted. Inez had not
been able to save a cent, all the earnings she kept went for art
supplies and to pay for her courses. She could never go back to
Aunt Ofelia, that was far worse than being with Joe. Sheila's
family lived in a crowded apartment in the projects . . . Inez
sighed, she wouldn't worry about all that now. She would find a
way. Maybe she could get financial aid or a student loan, perhaps a scholarship might give her enough money to set up a
place of her own near the school or even on campus. She didn't
know what to expect, but she did know she was going on to study.
The buzzer sounded and Inez took her break. Tonight she was
supposed to meet Aldo. The last time when they had met and
worked on the applications, she had wanted to tell him the truth.
He was the only friend she felt might be able to help her, advise
her in some way. But, Inez was afraid of what he would think of
her if he knew she was lying, and that there was no Frankie; it
might end their friendship. How could she tell him about Joe?
She just couldn't. She greeted a few of the other students as she
drank a seven-up and then went back to the studio to take her
second long pose of the evening.

Inez sat once again with her head bowed, leaning against the
back of her chair, with one arm down at the side, the other on her
right thigh and her knees slightly parted. She was deep in
thought and so it took her some time before she heard voices
shouting and a commotion in the studio. Startled, she looked up
when she heard Philip Johnson, the instructor shouting, "Who

the hell are you? Where the hell do you think you're going?" It took a few seconds before Inez could focus clearly and then her eyes met Joe Batista's. He was standing no more than a few feet in front of her, staring wide-eyed. Instinctively, she jumped up, put her hands over her breasts and crossed her legs.

In an instant, Joe lunged toward Inez, grabbing her long dark hair with both hands. She felt her head snap and then a sharp painful slap against the left side of her face and neck, just before she landed on the floor. She had fallen against several easels and stools. Inez tried to get up, but kept slipping against the mixture of oil and turpentine that had spilled on her and on the floor. Kicking and throwing aside whatever was in the way, Joe rushed toward her, trying to land a punch. Quickly Philip Johnson and some of the male students grabbed and leaned on Joe until they held him down.

"What the hell do you think you're doing here?" The instructor yelled. "What are you, a fucking madman?"

"I'm her husband . . ." Joe looked at Inez. "That's who I am! I'm married to that bitch . . . that whore is my wife!" He was choking with rage, trying to break loose from the grip of the men that held him tightly.

By now some students had helped Inez get up and she had found her way behind the screen. Her head was aching and she heard voices coming across the room like a faint buzz. Quickly, she took a towel, cleaned herself off as best she could and tried to control her trembling hands and fingers as she put on her clothes. The voices became louder and clearer.

"I'm her husband and she's my wife, you have no right to interfere."

"I don't give a fuck if you're her father. You can't come in here, disrupt my class and beat up on her."

"I got every right . . . she's mine!"

"Tough, buddy . . . we've already called the police. Explain it to them. This bastard's crazy."

"All I want is to take my wife home, that's all . . ."

"You are not touching her . . . and you can tell the cops your problems."

Inez had managed to put on her underwear and was now trying to get into her jeans and shirt. Several of the female students were standing outside the screen.

"He's crazy . . . did you see the way he hit her? Let's see if she's all right. She might need some help." A young woman poked her head in behind the screen. "Look, are you all right? Let us help you . . ."

"No . . . no, please," Inez interrupted. "Just, just let me alone. I mean . . . I'm okay. Thanks . . . really . . ."

"All right, but we're right here if you need us, and don't worry, he's not coming over here. They still have him pinned down."

"I'm not going to hit her, I tell you. Let me go! All I want to do is take my wife home. Let me go! Shit, she's mine. Mine! Do you hear?" Joe's screams made Inez shake so violently that she bent over afraid she might throw up. Her heart was beating so violently that she was afraid it might leap right out of her chest. Just then she felt someone put an arm around her.

"Come on . . . let's go, Inez." Without looking, she recognized Aldo's voice. He spoke in a whisper. "Now just shut your eyes and lean against me." Submissively, she did as she was told, closing her eyes and even put her hands over her ears. Aldo held her firmly as he led her discreetly out through the side door of the studio, down the stairs and out into the street. She took a deep breath, welcoming the fresh air.

"Taxi! Hey cabbie, over here!" Aldo's voice was sharp and clear. All during the ride Inez kept her eyes closed and her arms wrapped around Aldo. The sounds of traffic, the honking car horns, police sirens and screaming fire engines seemed like music to her, because she knew that she was going somewhere far away from Joe.

Inez finally opened her eyes as she stepped out of the cab. She stood in front of a large building that looked like a warehouse.

Inez followed Aldo up three long flights and waited until he unlocked the door.

"Here . . . come on in, Inez. This is my place. Sit, sit down here on the couch. That's it, lean back and put your feet up." He covered her with a blanket. "I'll get you a drink. Not gingerale this time . . . something stronger. You need it, okay?" Inez nodded.

She looked around her at a very large room with high ceilings and tall windows. It was possibly the biggest room she had ever seen anyone live in. It was filled with Aldo's large paintings. A couple of long work tables and a tremendous easel occupied most of the space. Off to the side was a makeshift a kitchen, with an old stove, refrigerator and several shelves stacked with pots and dishes. There was also a battered round oak table and several chairs. It smelled just like the League. Delicious smells, she thought, the smells of a working artist. Aldo returned with a glass.

"Here you go, Inez . . . some straight scotch. Drink up." Inez swallowed and coughed; it was a very strong taste. "Go on. Sip it slowly, it'll calm your nerves. Honest." Inez took a few sips and felt the warmth spread down into her gut and throughout her body. "Feeling better?"

"Yes," she paused. "I'm sorry, Aldo."

"It's okay."

"No, you don't understand. You see, there isn't any Frankie. I mean there is, but he's my brother and I haven't seen him since I was a kid. That man today, he's my husband. His name is Joe. I made up that story about Frankie . . . I'm sorry."

"I know. I figured out who he was. But look, it's okay, you got nothing to be sorry for."

"I'm just so ashamed . . .," Inez began to cry as feelings of shame and helplessness overwhelmed her.

"Shh . . . sh, it's okay. I understand. You don't owe me any explanations. Just lie down and rest. Look," he sat next to her, "stay here until you decide what to do next. You can sleep right here on the couch. I've got a loft bed up there . . ." Inez saw that at the far end of the room there was a ladder leading up to a platform with a bed. "Rest and take it easy. Tomorrow we can talk about it, okay? We can figure things out then."

"All right," Inez smiled weakly. He gave her a paper towel. She wiped her eyes and blew her nose. I really feel I should explain . . ."

"Tomorrow. Right now you're in no condition to explain anything. I'll get you some sheets, a pillow and more blankets." When Aldo returned, Inez reached out to him.

"Stay with me please . . . I don't want to be alone."

"Are you sure? You don't have to sleep with me."

"Please, don't leave me alone, not tonight." Aldo took Inez up to bed.

They made love several times. And that night Inez dreamt she was first on a roller coaster and then on a ship — later she was running — falling — walking. All night in her dreams, wherever Inez found herself and whatever she was doing, there was constant motion. It was as if she couldn't stand still, not even for one moment.

Part 5

After she turned twenty-one, Inez took time out from her busy life as a full-time student at Cooper Union and part-time job as a salesgirl, and filed for an annulment of her marriage to Joe Batista. She cited as grounds the fact that they had only lived together less than a year and had been separated for more than two years. She had even gathered up the courage to telephone Joe and accept his invitation to meet and talk — as old friends — he had said. When she told her friend Sheila Coleman that she was meeting Joe, Sheila became upset and wanted to go with her.

"I remember that guy's violent temper, Inez, and I don't think you should see him alone." But Inez had insisted on meeting him by herself.

"This is something I have to handle without anyone else, and then put it behind me. I want to see him, Sheila, face him and say what I have to. Sooner or later when he gets the papers for the annulment, he'll sign them, believe me. I'll be all right," she reassured her.

That afternoon, Inez tried to shake loose those remnants of fear that resurged when she thought of seeing Joe again. She tried not to give in to the feeling of intense apprehension as she left her small apartment on east 5th Street and walked west. They were meeting at a quiet restaurant in Soho. After all, a restaurant is a public place, she thought, Joe would think twice before becoming violent, and she could always call for help.

Inez blinked her eyes against the sting of the cold sharp winter wind, walking at a quick pace as she cut across the edge of Greenwich Village and headed south. After she had left him, Joe had gone on a rampage of rage and threats. He visited her friend Sheila and even Aunt Ofelia. First, he cried and pleaded that they help him get her back. Later, he made telephone threats and wrote nasty letters to them. Joe had even stationed himself out-side of Inez' office, until she finally had to quit and find another

job. When all these tactics failed, Joe had taken a semester off
from school and gotten a part-time job driving a cab so that he
could search all over New York City for Inez. The few times he
saw someone resembling Inez, he would follow the young
woman prepared for a confrontation and the use of force to bring
her back home. Each time he was disappointed. In fact, the
entire time he searched, he never once saw Inez. Finally he quit
his part-time job and went back to school.

For the first year, Inez walked around very frightened and
careful, always looking to the left, to the right and in back of her,
convinced that Joe was going to find her . . . but he never did. In
time, she stopped worrying about him and quite naturally went
about living her life.

But today, as she walked along ready to meet him, the memories of her life with him and his violent actions became vivid and
fresh in her mind. Inez recalled that even Aunt Ofelia had interfered, and written her a letter in care of Sheila. She had confessed she was afraid he might harm Inez. However, she also
wanted to know what Inez had done to provoke such a wonderful
man. Aunt Ofelia even offered to take Inez back if there were a
chance at reconciliation with Joe. At the time, Inez was out-
raged, but now she laughed and whispered into the cold winter
air, "that disgusting old witch!"

Inez finally reached the restaurant, took a deep breath,
squared her shoulders and walked in. The maitre d' greeted her.

"Pardon. Are you Mrs. Batista?" Inez winced when she
heard that name. "Are you?" She barely nodded.

"Come this way please. Your husband described you very
well. He's over there . . ." Inez followed him into a dimly lit
back room where most of the tables were empty. She saw Joe
seated at a booth. When he stood up to greet her, Inez was surprised. He appeared to be a smaller person than the one she
remembered and far less attractive.

"Hello, Inez . . ." As he leaned over to kiss her on the cheek,
Inez stepped away. "All right, I'm not going to touch you."

"May I take your coat, madam?" the maitre d' asked.

"No, thank you. I'll keep it." Inez took off her coat and draped it over her shoulders, then sat in the booth opposite Joe.

"Well," he smiled, "long time since we've been together. How are you?"

"I'm fine. How are you?"

"Great. I have another year before I get my law degree."

"Congratulations."

"From what I hear, you're in school too."

"Yes. This is my sophomore year." Joe grinned at her and pointed his finger as if admonishing her.

"You did all right for yourself, didn't you. Not bad for a little orphan."

"All right, I'm here Joe. What do you want?"

"No . . . what do you want, Inez?"

"You know what I want, an annulment. And I'll get it with or without you."

"Are you getting re-married?"

"No."

"Then, what's the rush?"

"That's my business, Joe."

The waiter appeared and they ordered lunch and drinks. Inez had a glass of white wine and Joe a double bourbon on the rocks.

"God damn it, Inez! You know you've gotten even more beautiful than ever. You've become some good looking woman. You still turn me on, baby." Joe reached over and put his hand on hers. Very slowly and deliberately she removed his hand. "What's the matter, you got somebody else? Somebody is doing it better than me . . . is that it? You think I don't know who you are and what you did. But I know, baby, and you got another thing coming to you. I know what you were doing and God knows with who . . ."

Inez watched Joe as he let loose a tirade of insults. She had forgotten just how distorted his face became. When he smiled, he gritted his teeth and grinned at her, then he would scowl, staring at her. She half heard what he was saying, because she knew he was about to make a scene. It all came back to her . . . how, in a while, after another drink, he would threaten her, try to frighten her and perhaps strike out. Inez recognized that, although she was apprehensive, she was no longer terrified of him, not anymore. She knew what she had to do and she waited.

". . . that's right! And I know you were fucking around while pretending to be a young innocent virgin wife. Don't try to deny it. I was even willing to forgive you after an army of guys saw you naked . . . but no, I wasn't good enough for you. You took me for a sucker, Inez, and I want you to know, nobody . . . nobody takes Joe Batista for a sucker. Why did you do it? Why? I gave you everything a woman could want. A home, food, everything. I took care of you . . . I really loved you and you stepped on my face. Why? Tell me . . . answer . . ." When Joe ordered a second drink, Inez was ready to answer him.

"You are right, Joe. I was seeing other men while I was married to you. And there is something else . . ." Inez paused a long moment, "I was sleeping with other men even before I met you. You see, I wasn't a virgin when I married you." Joe stared at her.

"What? What are you saying?"

"I wasn't a virgin when I married you," she repeated.

"What do you mean you weren't a virgin? How could that be? You never left your aunt's house without permission. I was the first man you ever dated . . . the first man to ever touch you. Remember? You didn't even know how to kiss. I had to teach you. Do you think I have a short memory? I was there on our wedding night. I was there! Remember what happened? I saw, and I know what happened. I was the first man to have you. Don't try to kid me, Inez. Don't play games with me."

"No, you weren't the first. On our wedding night . . . all that blood on the sheets the first time we had sex . . . everything, it was all contrived, I put it there."

"What? Wait a minute, you mean to tell me that wasn't blood? Get out of here . . . I know what I saw. That was blood! I've been around . . . I wasn't born yesterday."

"It was very easy to do, you know, a little mercurochrome and you never even noticed the difference."

"Are you serious?"

Inez permitted the slightest smirk to pass her lips but said nothing. "You mean to tell me that all them . . . that what happened . . ." Joe hesistated; he had heard stories like that, about women who fooled men. But that wasn't Inez. She couldn't have been that good an actress to deceive him like that. It just couldn't be. "All right, let's say you're saying the truth . . . I mean, who the hell did you sleep with, since you never went nowhere? How did . . ."

"With my uncle," Inez interrupted, "Uncle Generoso was my lover. That's right!"

"What? That old man?"

"That's right. And you know what? I was the one that seduced him. When we were in the house alone, I'd force myself on him. At first, he didn't want to do it . . . but then after a while, he wanted me. Then, after him, I got so used to doing it, that I began to have relations with my girlfriends' older brothers. I didn't stop there. Sometimes I'd pick up older guys in the movies and go with them to their cars. I've been having sex since I was about eleven." Inez sighed. "Now you know. I thought it's about time you knew the truth." Joe sat perfectly still, as if he were frozen in his seat. "Believe me," Inez added.

"Well," Joe cleared his throat, "I don't believe you." But Inez could see he was shaken.

"Suit yourself, Joe."

"You aren't telling me the truth, are you, Inez? You're putting me on."

"Why should I lie to you now? What difference does it make? I have no reason to put you on. None."

"Wait a minute." Joe shook his head as if trying to clear his mind. "Tell me something. Do you still do . . . the same thing today . . . I mean, now?"

"Uh huh," Inez nodded, "it's just the way I am . . . it's in my nature."

"You really fooled me, Inez. I mean this is very hard to believe. I mean, screwing around as a married woman is one thing, but doing it as a kid with your uncle . . . that's disgusting!" By now Joe was looking more sober than when she had first greeted him. "They have a word for women like you, you know that?" Joe looked all around him before he continued to speak, lowering his voice. "Nymphomaniacs. That's what they're called. I think that's what you are." Inez sipped her wine. They remained silent as Joe first frowned, then smiled observing her, trying to discern whether she was telling him the truth or playing a nasty joke on him. Inez smiled sweetly at Joe as she ate her salad. He barely touched his food. "Look," he spoke first. "Did you ever think of getting help? I'm sure they have some sort of treatment for that."

"Why? I like what I do. It's fun. Why should I change? You don't understand, Joe. You see, some people have all kinds of different hobbies: they play tennis, do photography, collect stamps . . . Me . . . I like sex, lots of sex. In a way, that's my hobby."

"You are sick, you know that? You are one real sick bitch! What about your Aunt Ofelia? I'll bet she doesn't even know. Does she?" Inez gave him a furtive glance and shrugged. "God . . . she probably did know all the time . . . and that's why she pushed so hard for us to get married. Is that what happened? Ofelia knew and wanted you out of her house and she saw me coming . . . a perfect patsy, *un pendejo*, a fucking pushover."

Inez held up her glass as if she were making a toast. "You are getting smart, Joe."

"So that was it! Then it's true? God, I wonder how many people knew what was going on? How many guys saw the horns on my head? How many men in the old neighborhood humped you and laughed at me? What a jerk I've been. To think I was so in love with you. What a sucker . . . *que come-mierda* . . . what a fool . . ." Joe buried his face in his hands. Inez watched him cautiously, tempted to put on her coat and run out. She was afraid that she had gone too far and that he might at any moment look up and throw a punch at her. But, she held her ground, remaining seated, and waited. After what seemed to her to be hours instead of minutes, he looked up and spoke in a hoarse whisper.

"Tell me one thing . . . I only want to know one thing from you. When you married me, did you want to . . . reform? I mean, did you love me and feel I could help you? Make you respectable? I have to know this." Inez waited hesitating — just for a second. She actually pitied him. "You have to tell me the truth. I'm entitled to that much. After all, I am your husband. What were your feelings for me? Did you marry me with intentions of being mine . . . only mine?"

"I . . . I didn't. No, I had no intentions of reforming or changing my ways. I was never in love with you, Joe. I'm sorry, but that's the truth."

"No . . . noooo . . ." Joe Batista whimpered, "oh, God." He began to sob, "oh, God . . ." The few people seated in the dining room turned to look at him. As she watched Joe sobbing uncontrollably, Inez slipped on her coat and motioned to the waiter.

"Is everything all right?" the waiter asked.

"I think we'll be leaving now," said Inez, "please bring the check." The waiter hesitated. "Please, there is nothing you can do, just bring the check," Inez insisted. By now Joe had stopped crying and was wiping his eyes and blowing his nose into a napkin. The waiter put the check down in front of Joe, as the maitre d' arrived looking worried.

"Can I get you anything else, sir? Has everything been satisfactory?"

"Everything is fine," Joe said and took a sip of water. "I'm all right, thanks."

Outside of the restaurant, it was dark and bitter cold, Inez and Joe stood facing each other.

"I don't know whether to kill you or just walk away!" Joe grimaced and clenched his fists. "You are nothing but a piece of trash . . . the worst kind of whore, a low life *puta*!" He lifted his right hand and made a fist threatening Inez. In spite of the fear she felt, as her insides trembled, Inez stood perfectly still and looked directly at Joe. "Bitch!" he yelled as he punched his right fist into his left palm. "You know . . .," he glared at her, "I don't know whether you are telling me the truth or not . . . I'm still not sure. But I know one thing, you are not worth another minute of my time. Whore! I never ever want to see you again. You can fucking drop dead for all I care!" Joe turned and walked away so rapidly that he seemed to be running. She watched until he disappeared around a corner.

Inez looked up at the sky: thin clouds obscured a full moon. She waited until the moon appeared illuminating clouds and silhouetting rooftops against the dark blue sky. She stretched out her arms and inhaled, filling her lungs with the cold brisk night air. Then, Inez turned, spun herself around and around and skipped a few times before she headed for home.